S0-BFD-385

Armadillo
Recon Unit

Armadillo Recon Unit

and other Tall Tales

Bil Lepp

Quarrier Press
Charleston, WV

Quarrier Press
Charleston, WV

Copyright 2004, Bil Lepp

All rights reserved. No part of this book may be
reproduced in any form or means, electronic or
mechanical, including photocopying, recording, or by
any information storage and retrieval system, without permission in writing from the publisher.

Book and cover design:
Colleen Anderson/Mother Wit

ISBN: 1-891852-38-8

Library of Congress Catalog Card Number:
2004111869

10 9 8 7 6 5 4 3 2 1

Cover painting by Erin Turner

Printed in the United States of America

Distributed by:
Pictorial Histories Distribution
1125 Central Ave.
Charleston, WV 25302
www.wvbookco.com

To Ellie and Noah

Table of Contents

1. The Butti Mystery 1

2. Thinking Behind 16

3. The Ultra-Secret Advanced Armadillo
   Reconnaissance Unit 26

4. Vanity PL8 31

5. Avant Garden 39

6. Something in the Water 41

7. Fat Bats 51

8. Naaman and the Hiccups 60

9. Artist's Renderings 65

10. The Fall of Babble-On 75

11. Quantity 4: Quality 0 81

12. Stop Sign Man 87

13. A Ride in the Pinpricked Hyphen 92

14. The Art of No-Hope Fishing 98

15. Jonah, The Last Two Chapters 103

16. Dimes 107

17. Animal Escort 114

18. Of Chicken Wieners and Fathers-in-Law 120

19. Engine Blockhead 125

20. Falsecium Abidebyme: Part I? 129

21. Deerly Departed -By Paul Lepp 144

22. The Stealth Catfish - By Paul Lepp 148

About the Stories 151

The Butti Mystery

New rumors about Bigfoot had started up again late last fall. There had always been stories passed around in Halfdollar about a Bigfoot, but nothing very reliable. But last fall, no less a respectable citizen and outdoorsman than Old Man Sullivan had reported to the crowd at Billy the Kid's Tombstone, the local tavern, that he himself had seen massive tracks in the mud by a stream he was fishing. He said it couldn't have been a bear or a man, and he doubted it was an ape or anything like that. Old Man Sullivan had said the word, *Bigfoot*. The rumor mill soon became littered with reports of sightings and tracks in the woods.

Skeet and I were skeptical, but vigilant nonetheless. As a rule, we didn't believe in Bigfoot, but a fellow couldn't be too careful. Nobody wanted to engage in hand-to-hand combat with a mythical creature of great strength and intelligence. Skeet and I already had the odds stacked against us when it came to the double whammy of strength and intelligence.

The rumors wilted a bit during the holiday season, but started up anew in mid-January. This time, Sheriff Hasbro told us about a sighting. While we sat quietly, albeit unwillingly, in the back of his patrol car after running a snowmobile, accidentally, through the ice atop the deep end of the city pool, Hasbro told us that a large hairy beast was recently spotted rummaging in the city dump.

"Sheriff," I scolded from the backseat, "you should be more careful when you go to the dump."

"And you," he glowered, "should be more careful when you ride your snowmobile 'accidentally' up the high-dive ladder."

"Did the beast leave any tracks?" asked Skeet.

"Just a few big footprints. I had Old Man Sullivan take a look. He said they were just like the ones he saw up on the creek last fall."

By February, winter had settled into our blood and slowed our adventurous metabolisms to a crawl. The days were cold, dark, and boring. Our memories from summer and fall were used up, and prospects for warm weather escapades were far off, somewhere on the other side of mid-March. We got up in the dark morning, walked to school with the streetlights still on, and by the time we got out of school the sun had already set. It was a miserable way to spend week after week, locked inside a torturous classroom the entire time that the sun was visible. Even teacher-baiting lost some of its luster. The only good argument we had got going in weeks was with Mr. Hundfoss, our English teacher.

"Synonyms," he said, "are words that share the same or similar meanings, like 'tizzy' and 'tantrum.' Antonyms are words with opposite meanings, like 'purify' and 'taint.'"

Skeet raised his hand and said smugly, "And 'tizzy' is an antonym of 'taint.'"

Mr. Hundfoss looked at Skeet awkwardly. "What in the world are you talking about, Mr. Barth?"

"Well," said Skeet, winking at a nearby girl, "I'll use them in a sentence. Let's say one guy is asking a second guy if a third guy is insane. The first guy might say, 'Tis he crazy'? And the second guy would answer, 'No, he t'aint.'" Skeet smiled triumphantly as the class broke out in laughter.

Mr. Hundfoss balled up his fists as his face turned pink. "All right, Mr. Barth," he said quietly, "that'll be enough of that." He cleared his throat. "Now then, a homonym is when two words are spelled or pronounced the same, but have different meanings."

Without raising my hand, I asked, "So are synonyms antonyms of homonyms?"

Mr. Hundfoss momentarily lost control of his cheek muscles. "Well," he said slowly, giving the matter some thought, "I guess so. I guess you could say that. Why do you ask?"

"Um," I said, "I was just wondering."

"I don't get it," Mr. Hundfoss said, taking a step backward. "Where's the joke?"

"Honest," I said, "I was just asking. Trying to learn."

He straightened his belt, tugged on his sweater, "I'm watching you, Lepp. There's something in that question that is supposed to foul me up, but I'm on to you."

The class began giggling.

"See!" he shouted. "I don't get it, but I bet it's dirty." He was pointing at me, glaring.

Skeet asked, "What are some other synonyms?"

Caught off guard, Mr. Hundfoss jerked his head toward Skeeter. "Well," he said, pulling his sweater down again, "I suppose 'but' and 'yet' are synonymous."

"I don't think so," replied Skeet.

"What?" asked Hundfoss. "Do you have a degree in English?"

"No," answered Skeet, "but I think 'yet' suggests something positive, while 'but' implies a negative."

"I think the two words are interchangeable, but if you're so sure, give me an example," said Hundfoss smugly.

Skeet leaned back in his chair while Hundfoss

walked around his desk, opened the center drawer, pulled out a bottle of antacids, and swallowed two. "Well?" he asked Skeet, "have you come up with an example where 'but' and 'yet' are not synonyms?"

Skeet said, "Not but, yet I'm thinking."

Hundfoss fell into his chair. "Mr. Barth," he said after a moment, "you are not funny. The grade you are getting in this class is not funny. You are clever, I'll give you that, but, speaking grammatically, I seriously doubt that you, or your friend Mr. Lepp, could put an asterisk on your colon if you had two 'ands' and a 'but'"!

The class sat silent, stunned at Hundfoss' sudden wit. And then everyone, including Skeet and Hundfoss, laughed brightly. It wasn't much, but it gave us that much more reason and courage to press on toward spring.

On the way out of class Hundfoss stopped us and said, "Look, you boys need a little extra credit in this class. You're supposed to graduate at the end of this term. The whole town hopes you both will get accepted to colleges far away from here. I will do anything I can for this town and its dreams. It would be so nice if you boys went to college in Iraq, or Siberia, or North Korea, or some such. But you need to pass this class to do it. So, I'll give you a chance. You boys write me a paper, a ten page paper, on any subject you want, and I'll make sure you pass my class with flying colors."

"Siberia would be neat," I said to Skeet.

"Yeah, they have tigers there," he said.

"And the Yeti," Hundfoss injected.

"That's it." Skeet shouted, "we'll write a paper on the Yeti that Old Man Sullivan saw."

Forced to endure the tripartite hardships of indoor activities, school, and a research paper, Skeet and I took a drastic step. We went to the public library. We had decided that with nothing else to do, and no real adventures to be had, we might as well look up Bigfoot in the library and find out what we could.

As we stepped in the door of the public library, Mrs. Phist jerked involuntarily. She looked at her desk calendar and croaked, "You're early. You boys don't usually invade this building until after Valentine's Day."

"It's been a hard winter, Mrs. Phist," I said apologetically.

"We won't be any trouble," Skeet added.

Mrs. Phist snorted. "The first peep I hear out of you and I call the Sheriff. You didn't bring those little fishing poles did you?" she asked.

We shook our heads. This question was in reference to the time Skeet and I had learned that there were microfiche at the library. It was an embarrassing, if understandable, error on our part.

"We need books on the Bigfoot," Skeet said proudly.

"Glory be." Mrs. Phist said, her hand going to her chest. "What on earth for?"

"Were doing some research on the rumors, and writing a paper for Mr. Hundfoss." Skeet answered.

"Well, you CANNOT do any experiments in here." It was always satisfying to make a librarian shout, especially before we had done anything but request materials.

Mrs. Phist knew better than to send us to the card catalog. It was quicker and less painful for her to just pull up the call numbers we needed on her computer and point us in the general direction of the books. This time though, she seemed to be one step ahead of us. She had a pile of books and articles about Bigfoot on the counter behind her desk.

"Lucky for you," she said, "I just happen to have a whole collection of materials right here." She patted the pile, and then handed them over to us.

After about an hour of reading, Skeet finally said, "There has never been a reliable sighting of the Bigfoot in these parts. They're all out west or up in Canada."

"And the Yeti," I added, "seems to only show up in Asia. So what we have here, if the rumors can be believed, is an as yet undiscovered breed of Sasquatch."

"I guess we get to name it," said Skeet. "I mean, we are doing the initial study. We might even get to write the story for *National Geographic*. So we better come up with a good name."

We sat quietly, thinking.

"I've got it," Skeet said, slapping the table. "The Butti."

"The Butti?" I asked.

"Yep. Because its like the Yeti, but not exactly like it. What we have is a creature synonymous with the Bigfoot and the Yeti. So, we call it the Butti."

"How do we spell it? I mean, if it's just a combination of the words, that would be B-E-T-I. And that would be pronounced 'Betty'. We can't have people thinking this terrible monster is named Betty. It wouldn't strike fear into their hearts. People might think it's gentle, approach it, and get hurt."

"I see what you mean. And we can't spell it B-U-T-I, because people would think it was 'Beauty,' and that's no name for a monster," Skeet added.

We sat a bit longer. Finally, from the desk across the room, Mrs. Phist said, "B-U-T-T-I. And don't giggle because I spelled 'butt.'"

"No, ma'am," I said. "No, that's a great way to spell it. 'Butti.'"

We had our beast named. We knew his habits. Now we just had to find him.

•••••

"Could it be," I whispered to Skeeter, "that something spilled?"

"What could have spilled?" he hissed back.

"Maybe," Skeet said, "a canteen spilled."

"Did you bring a canteen into the tent?" I asked.

"No. Did you?" Skeet said.

"No. Did Rudy?" I hinted.

Rudy was Skeeter's nine year-old cousin. He was visiting with Skeets' family, and Skeeter's mother had forced us to take Rudy with us on our overnight Butti expedition. We were eighteen-years-old and having a kid half our age along was not our idea of relaxing. First of all, Mrs. Barth had made us leave our guns at home so we wouldn't shoot Rudy. Camping was all right all by itself, and we enjoyed the break from home, but hunting was better. And there was, after all, a Bigfoot on the loose in the area.

The fact that the temperature was supposed to drop below zero during the night hadn't really bothered us. We liked to test our camping skills. But now, with the sun creeping over the mountaintops and our breath hanging in the tent, we were becoming frustrated. Somehow, during the night, the floor of the tent had become coated with liquid, and then, subsequently, with ice. Our sleeping bags, we had discovered, were frozen solid to the floor of the tent and neither of us could get our arms out of our tight mummy bags. We were stuck. Rudy was snoring contentedly by the door.

"So?" Skeet said, "What could have spilled?"

"Besides your cousin? I don't know," I retorted.

"What are you trying to say?"

"I'm trying to say, could your cousin have, well, is there any chance that we are lying in his frozen. . ."

From somewhere outside the tent came the sound of frozen bushes being pushed apart. This was followed by feet crunching in the snow and the snort of a rooting animal.

Rudy woke up with a jolt and screamed a long,

blood-thawing, "AAAAAAAAAAAAAAAAAAAA-
AAAAAAAAAAAAAAA!" There was a terrifying ripping as he lurched up, bending at the hips until his
head hit his toes. He couldn't have looked more like a
human mouse trap slapping shut if he had tried. The
back of his sleeping bag, which was just as frozen to
the floor as ours, ripped loose from the rest of the sleeping bag and lay in the ice, light blue fabric held fast by
light blue ice, with tiny down feathers frozen in the ice,
swaying in the disturbed air. And then, with a screech-
ing like a nail coming out of a board, Rudy pulled himself free of the ruined bag, unzipped the tent, and ran
shrieking toward home.

"Well," Skeeter said, "he might have at least had the
courtesy to say good-bye."

"Or at least zip the tent back up." I added.

"Did you notice that he was fully dressed? Shoes
and everything? Did he sleep like that?" Skeet wondered out loud.

We lay there, frozen to the floor of a new tent in
new sleeping bags, with the flap open, snow blowing
in on top of us as the sun rose, and Rudy's cries causing avalanches to rumble down nearby mountains. The
rooting noises outside had ceased.

"I don't want to die here, like this, but I'll be darned
if I am going to sit up and tear my new mummy bag," I
said.

"Me too," agreed Skeet.

"Maybe if we lay here long enough the bags will
thaw," I suggested.

We lay quietly for a few minutes and then Skeet
asked: "What do you suppose got into Rudy? A night-
mare or something?"

"I'm less worried about what *got into* Rudy than
about what *got out* of Rudy, and thus what we are frozen in," I said.

"Maybe we shouldn't have told him about the Butti," Skeet said.

"We had to. He's a kid. You're supposed to scare them on camping trips," I opined.

The bushes outside rustled again, the snow crunched, and the rooting and grunting came close to the tent.

"I hope," I whispered, "that that is not a skunk out there." I wiggled my shoulders and knees quietly, hoping to break free of the ice.

"If it's a bear we can just play dead. If it's a skunk, I'm going to get out of here, sleeping bag and all," Skeet whispered back.

We lay still. The rooting continued.

Trying to say it with a laugh, I said, "You don't reckon it's the Butti, do you?"

I heard Skeet jerk around in his bag. He forced a laugh and said, "No. There's no such thing."

Something brushed against the tent wall, about two feet off the ground, to the left of the open door. It was a large something. I swallowed hard. There was a snuffling, and then the frozen breath of a large beast, carried on the breeze, drifted in a thick cloud through the open door of the tent. I swallowed harder. The large something moved just to the edge of the open door and grunted. I swallowed my hardest, so hard that I pulled a muscle in my neck and my Adam's apple nearly turned to applesauce.

I lay perfectly still, except for my uncontrollable shivering, with my eyes shut hard. Skeet was scared stiff, which, under the circumstances, was the best way to be scared. If it was a bear, Skeet would appear dead. I would look to the bear like a nervous pig in a poke. After a few moments I carefully opened one eye, and then screamed, "BUTTIIIIIIIIIIIIIIIIII!"

When my scream died down, and I calmed enough

to see straight, I saw that the hairy face of the Butti disappeared into a checked, wool hunting coat. Odd. And then I heard Skeet say, "Oh. Hello, Mr. Sullivan. What are you doing up here? Your winter beard is coming along nicely."

Old Man Sullivan raised a gloved hand and stroked his beard. "Thanks," he said, "I was thinking that very thing myself. So, besides screaming bloody murder, what are you boys doing up here?"

"Oh," Skeet said, "just camping."

"Why are you still in bed? You're missing the best part of the day," he asked.

"Well," Skeet said, trying to shrug, "we're sort of, well, frozen in place."

Old Man Sullivan studied on the problem for a few minutes, muttered to himself, and then lit a fire. He rummaged in our gear until he found a cook pot, heated some water, and then carefully poured the warm water under our sleeping bags. The ice thawed quickly and we hopped out of the bags, changed into dry clothes, and then expressed our thanks to Sullivan. We leaned our now refreezing bags against a tree.

"What was that you yelled when I stuck my head in the tent?" Old Man Sullivan asked me.

"Oh, that." I said, "Butti."

"And what, pray tell, does Butti mean?" he asked.

We explained the origin of the species. While we talked, Sullivan seemed to study us with great interest. Then he nodded his head, said, "Hum," and stroked his beard. He patted his rifle and said, "Well, if I see the Butti out here I'm not going to take any chances. Those tracks I saw were huge. This Butti ain't no beast to be toyed with." Then he stood, nodded at us, and walked off into the woods.

"Well," Skeet said, "no sense sticking around here. We can't camp tonight with the sleeping bags frozen.

We might as well take down the tent, pack up, and then explore for the day. We'll come back at dusk, get our gear and head home."

We piled everything together and then headed off into the cold, cold morning. After a while it occurred to us that Rudy had run off into the woods alone, and that he might not know his way home. "And," Skeet added, "there's the Butti to consider. What if Rudy runs into him?"

"You'd have one less annoying little cousin." I said.

"And one mad mother, and one mad aunt."

"We'd better make sure he made it home."

We turned in our tracks, grabbed our gear at the camp, and followed Rudy's footprints toward town. After about a mile, another set of prints joined Rudy's. It swept in from a thick clump of pine trees and then paralleled Rudy's tracks. The prints were sunk deep in the snow, were at least eighteen inches long, and had five toes with claws extending from each digit. And whatever it was, it walked on two feet.

"Holy cow!" Skeet yelled.

"The Butti!" I yelled.

"We should have brought a camera," Skeet lamented.

We doubled our pace, followed the two sets of prints around a bend and then stopped in our tracks. Rudy's prints disappeared. All that was left were the big tracks of the Butti, and they left the trail and headed into the woods.

"Uh-oh," Skeet muttered.

We quickly turned and tracked the Butti into the woods, expecting at any moment to find the bones of the little kid stuffed under a bush. Amazingly, after about two hundred yards, Rudy's tracks reappeared, as though the Butti had dropped him. Rudy's tracks slid back toward the trail, and the Butti's continued deeper into the woods.

"He got away," Skeet said.

"I wonder if he's hurt," I added.

"Gosh," Skeet lamented, "I really want to follow the Butti's tracks, but I guess we'd better check on Rudy."

"We can come back tomorrow and follow the Butti, "I suggested.

Rudy's tracks made it all the way home, and we found him in the kitchen, being nursed by Skeet's mother and aunt. He was pale and spent. After a few minutes, he recounted the tale of how he had been running along toward the house when a giant, ape-like beast had rushed up behind him, snatched him up, and carried him off into the woods.

"How come he didn't eat you?" Skeet asked, only to be slapped in the back of his head by his mother.

"I d-d-d-d-don't know," Rudy answered, unsteadily.

"Did you pester him with questions while he was carrying you off to certain doom?" Skeet asked, and was again slapped.

"N-n-n-n-n-no. I just screamed and screamed," Rudy said.

"That would do it," I said, mostly just to see if Mrs. Barth would slap me. She did.

There was a knock at the door. Mrs. Barth had called Sheriff Hasbro, and he brought Old Man Sullivan. They questioned Rudy for some time. They finally decided that he had not made up the story and that we were not responsible for the episode, thanks to Old Man Sullivan who vouched that he had spoken with us for some time after Rudy had run off. "No way they could have done it," he concluded.

It was a sad thing to be the town's best troublemakers and not even be suspected of causing the biggest ruckus in recent memory.

The snow fell hard that night, covering the tracks of

the Butti. There was no way to follow him. We stayed near the house all that day. When the evening newspaper came out the headline read, "Visiting Youngster Abducted by Butti."

"Ain't that just a fine thing," Skeet said, "Rudy freezes us to the floor of the tent and then gets in the newspaper just because a mythical beast almost ate him."

"Yeah," I said. "And they used the term 'Butti' without so much as mentioning that we made the phrase up."

The article went on to say that the Town Council would hold a private meeting the next night to discuss the Butti problem.

Skeet and I sat silent for a long time, pondering.

"We have to catch it," Skeet said at last, "if we want to get any credit from the whole deal."

I agreed. We pondered quietly some more.

Skeet suddenly stiffened. He jerked his head toward me, his eyes big and white. "I heard my mother on the phone when she was inviting my aunt and Rudy to come down," he said.

"So?" I asked.

"I remember, she said 'We're trying to keep the boys out of trouble. Winter gets them all worked up and bored. Can you and Rudy come down, for a little surprise?'" he recounted.

"It was surprising enough," I said, "springing that runt on us like they did."

"No," Skeet said emphatically, "think about it."

I thought. And then I smiled. "I think I know how to catch the Butti."

"Me too," he whispered, "let's go."

We went. We were out until very late, gathering our gear and setting our trap. We stayed quiet all the next day, watching TV. Fifteen minutes after the private Town

Council meeting started, we burst through the doors of City Hall. The members of the Town Council watched as Skeet walked to the front of the room. Proudly, Skeet announced, "Ladies and gentlemen of the Council, we have presently captured the Butti!"

Gasps escaped from all the members of the Council.

"Just what are you boys up to?" asked Sheriff Hasbro.

"Lights!" Skeet yelled.

I had remained in the back of the room, waiting for this command. I switched off the lights, sending the Council Room into pitch blackness. And then I pulled a cord, releasing the huge cargo net Skeet and I had bought from Sullivan's Flea Market some time ago. The net fell from where we had suspended it under a false ceiling, and landed with a thump. There were muffled screams and curses from the Council.

I turned the lights back on. All the members of the Town Council– Sheriff Hasbro, Old Man Sullivan, Mrs. Phist, Mr. Hundfoss, and Mrs. Barth, looked out at us from beneath the net.

I walked up to Skeet, who just shook his head at the Council members.

Skeet said, "I am ashamed of all of you. Surely you could have come up with a better way to keep us out of trouble than to invent the Butti. I'll admit, it was a clever plan, having Old Man Sullivan start the rumor way back in autumn, getting us mindful of the idea, and then to slowly, but steadily keep reminding us. But to involve Rudy, a child? Shame on you. Someone could have gotten hurt." He shook his head again.

The Council members studied their hands and the tabletop from beneath the net.

"Mr. Hundfoss," I asked, "do we still owe you a paper?"

He glanced up, then at the members of the Council,

then at us. Softly, he said, "No, I don't suppose so."

"Well then," Skeet said, "I guess we'll just go see what we can get into."

"Just one last thing," I said. "Why did you freeze us to the floor of the tent?"

Old Man Sullivan smiled. Laughing, he said, "We didn't, that was all Rudy's doing. What you might call an accident, brought on by too much hot chocolate, and fear."

"I knew it!" I shouted at Skeet. "My brand new sleeping bag!"

And then we left the Butti, trapped and chagrined, but wiser for its efforts. If left alone, the Butti would be far more dangerous come next winter, but Skeeter and I were now old enough to vote, and the town elections were just a few months away.

As it turns out, the Butti is a mythical creature able to strike fear and politics into the hearts of even the most apathetic constituents.

Thinking Behind

There have been many times in my life when it has occurred to me all too late to think ahead, to think a thing through before committing an act. That is to say, instead of thinking ahead, I often find myself thinking behind, which explains why I accomplish most things by the seat of my pants. I am not the first behind-thinker in the world, and will likely not be the last. Many of the most remarkably unaccomplished people throughout history have been our greatest behind-thinkers. Most of them suffered heinous, untimely deaths, but their contributions to society have been invaluable.

Where, for example, would the English language be without such phrases as, "Oh golly . . . this is gonna hurt," or "What was I thinking?" These phrases were doubtlessly the last words of two fine behind-thinkers. But the contributions don't end there. Without behind-thinkers we would probably never have come up with the statement, "You have the right to remain silent." Without behind-thinkers there would be far fewer jails, which means thousands of people who make their living from the penal system would be out of work. Guards, wardens, cooks, prison bus drivers, all would be looking for a way to feed their families if it weren't for skilled behind-thinkers plying their trade, day in and day out. Not to mention all the folks on the cop dramas on TV. Cop shows make up about half of all TV programming, so think of all the actors, writers, producers, grips . . . They would all be jobless if it weren't for behind-thinkers. You just can't have TV without criminals. And, finally, how would we know not to smoke while pumping gas, run with scissors, or golf during an electrical storm if it were not for the careless, irresponsible, loveable behind-thinkers who came before us?

I took an auto mechanic's class at our local tech school last winter, mostly just for something to do. As a consequence, I now know a bit about engine repair. I say that this is a consequence because I got a C- in the class. I thus feel compelled to do my own work on my cars. This usually results in my having to have a car towed from the greatest possible distance. Getting a C- in a mechanic's class is like a C- in a midwife class, or flight school. People have no confidence in your abilities, but in a jam, you're the only person around with any know-how. But everybody knows how things are going to end.

After I "fixed" our cars several times, Paula got sick of it. She finally went over to her uncle's farm and talked him into giving her a clunker. Her uncle sort of collected abandoned vehicles. He won them in bets, traded for them, bought them, or people just left them in his yard like unwanted pets. As a result, he possessed many cars that had not been registered to anybody since long before the dawn of the computer age and thus did not technically exist. No one knew for sure how Uncle made his living. But if you paid attention to his stock of cars and the news, you would occasionally see a car that was the getaway car in a bank heist or the like, which greatly resembled a car that had recently vanished from Uncle's farm.

Paula got me an old Escort to work on whenever I

got the urge to play mechanic. You put a C- mechanic up against a C- car and, well, a certain mutual bond forms. You get a double negative in mechanical form. To everyone's surprise—myself included—I accidentally got the car running. I never registered the car, because I never had any intention of driving it on the road.

It's a sporty 1985, four-door, hatchback job, with front-wheel drive. What it is not, is an off-road vehicle. Nevertheless, the other day I needed to move some things from the shed in our backyard to a new storage shed on the other side of our property. I drove the Escort into the backyard, parked it in the grass, and began the loading process. I was basically just taping up some boxes and moving them to the car. It was raining though, and each time I carried a box to the car, rainwater would run down my wrists, nearly up to my elbows. My forearms were freezing, so I took some of the packing tape and wrapped a couple of tight loops around the cuffs of my jacket. That sealed out the rain just fine.

The job didn't take long, but . . . it took long enough. When I got back in the Escort, started it up, put it in gear, and hit the gas, well, the wheels just spun and spun. Being stuck in the mud is one of those situations where the brain just naturally shuts down. One of two things happens. You either cry, or you jump to the conclusion that you are not really stuck and that if you just put the pedal to the metal the car will jump out of the mud and you will be fine. Well, I'm not given to crying, so I floored it. I figured that if worse came to worse, the front wheels would dig a hole all the way to China and, with any luck, it would not be raining there. I'd just get some traction in good old Beijing and drive home. I didn't make it to China. When the oil pan hit the grass, my mind kicked back into gear.

I got out of the car, walked to the front of the house, got in our four-wheel drive Jeep, and backed it into the backyard. I parked it in front of the Escort, hooked a tow rope from the back of the Jeep to the front of the Escort, put the Escort in neutral, climbed back in the Jeep, engaged the four-wheel drive, and effortlessly pulled the Escort out of the mud.

I was feeling right fine about the whole adventure until I realized that I was suddenly driving two cars at once, connected only by a fifteen foot tow rope, with one car directly behind the other. As a person regularly accused of being unfit to drive even one vehicle at a time, I was in a bind.

A lot of strange and varied things cross your mind, few of them useful or calming, when you realize that you are driving two cars at once. This is a classic behind-thinker's predicament. The first thing that crossed my mind was, "Wow! I never noticed how steep this backyard really is." The next thought I had was, "Huh, that's odd. When I hit the brakes in the Jeep, it seems to have no effect on the Escort's rate of speed." In fact, I discovered that the slower I drove the Jeep, the faster the Escort seemed to be coming up behind me, directly behind me.

Let me back up a second here and explain why I was engaged in this exercise all alone in the first place. You see, I try to be a good husband and not bother my wife anymore than I have to. It was late at night, maybe 11:00, and, as I said, raining hard. Paula was inside, warm and snug. When the Escort got stuck I thought, "Well, I'll be a good husband and get it out of the mud myself. Won't Paula be pleased that I got the car unstuck all by myself, without her having to come out and get soaked." That was then. Presently, I was thinking about how I was going to explain to Paula that I wrecked two cars in one fell swoop. I doubted that it would go over well. "Honey," I would say, "I just wrecked both cars, but the good news is, you didn't have to get drenched in the process."

In our nine years of marriage I'd had to admit worse things, with even less good news attached, but I still didn't figure she'd be happy about it.

All of this was passing through my head as the Escort was rushing toward the rear end of the Jeep. All that, and what I would tell my insurance man. I know that if you rear-end someone it is always your fault, but how could I be liable for rear-ending myself if I wasn't actually driving the car I rear-ended myself with?

At last, it dawned on me that slowing the Jeep wouldn't necessarily slow the Escort because the brake lines did not, due to gross manufacturer oversight, pass from the Jeep to the Escort through the towline. Man, if I got out of this, I was going to sue whoever invented the towrope. What an incompetent rube.

Seconds before impact, I floored the Jeep and shot away from the oncoming Escort, narrowly avoiding rear-ending myself. I had just managed to prove the old saying, "If I was the last guy on earth, there'd be some moron braking in front of me."

The towrope collected its slack off the ground—as I sped away from the Escort—and went positively rigid between the two cars. There was a tremendous jolt as the Jeep began pulling again. With the rope rigid, I naturally braked again, figuring the rigid line would slow the Escort. No good. The line went limp.

To complicate matters, as though they needed further complications, I was running out of backyard. Very soon I was going to have to make a right turn out of the yard and onto the driveway. But it was no ordinary right turn. No sir, I had to drive through two trees, which was difficult enough in one car, and at two miles per hour. I could tell that it was going to be even harder while driving two cars at fifty miles per hour. I'd have to thread the Jeep through the narrow hole, drive straight for as long as possible to get the Escort through, and then turn hard and fast enough to sling the Escort around before it ploughed through the fence on the far side of the drive, and into the cow pasture.

I made it through the trees without a hitch and then slung the Escort so hard that it went up on two wheels. I was watching it in the rearview mirror as it skidded across the drive toward the fence. I have to admit, I was pretty impressed with myself, harboring thoughts of becoming a stunt driver. I mean, I could really drive that Escort on just those two wheels. It straightened out just before the fence and everything was going fine. Then, I took my eyes off the rearview mirror and looked again out the windshield. We were headed straight toward the house, and it was far too late to stop. I was seconds away from wrecking both cars *and* the house. If the pending wreck didn't hurt Paula, she'd kill me.

I had no choice. I jerked the wheel of the Jeep around as hard as I could, doing a tight U-turn. Now I was headed straight at myself in the Escort. Only, I wasn't in the Escort. I flicked the steering wheel of the Jeep and managed to slip by the Escort. If I hadn't still been driving the Escort on just the two wheels, I never would have made it by.

I felt the jolt as the Escort was jerked suddenly around, and the bounce as it landed on all four wheels. It regained its pursuit. I came out of the driveway onto County Road 513 at a frightening speed, following myself closely in the Escort. As we started down a hill, the Escort began creeping up on my left, getting closer and closer. There was no slowing it. I was a mad man back there. We went into a curve and the Escort edged up on the inside. For a moment, I was beside myself, but then I got out of my way and let myself pass. The Escort drifted out ahead of the Jeep.

The moment the car you are towing drifts in front of the car you are driving, well, that's trouble enough. But there's more. You see, I'm a very competitive person, and this was beginning to look like a race, and I don't like to lose. Furthermore, the Jeep is a much better car than that Escort, and I couldn't let the lesser car win. I just wouldn't be able to face myself if I let myself lose to myself while I was driving both cars in the race, but wasn't driving the car I was losing to. It was driving me crazy. I put the pedal to the metal. The Jeep soared out in front of the Escort.

Do you know what a lay-over road is? It is a very common type of road in West Virginia. It is essentially a two-way, one lane road built where it would be nearly impossible to fit a two-lane road. Sometimes a lay-over will stretch itself and become a one-and-half-lane road, or narrow to a three-quarter lane road, but generally it is a solid one lane road with occasional turn-outs, wide shoulders, driveways, or shallow ditches. Driver etiquette on a lay-over road is simple. When two cars meet, the driver nearest a wide spot, without having to back up, pulls over, or lays-over and stops, giving the other driver room to pass. Any road in West Virginia, barring interstate highways, can suddenly, without warning, become a lay-over. County Road 513 changes from a two-lane, divided road, into a lay-over road about three miles from my house.

As I approached the beginning of the lay-over road, with the Jeep way out ahead of the Escort, I noticed headlights coming toward me. I couldn't slow down, for fear that I'd hit myself in the rear, and I couldn't just charge on, because then I would collide with the oncoming car and rear-end the Jeep. I got to a wide spot, worked the steering wheel of the Jeep, and managed to fling the Escort from behind me. It slid across the road and dropped halfway into the ditch. I dropped part way into the ditch on my side of the road, and the oncoming car shot between the Jeep and the Escort, with inches to spare on either side. I looked in the rear-view mirror and saw brake lights blazing from the just passed car. Well, that was natural. The guy probably needed to change his underwear.

And then I saw the flashing blue lights of a police vehicle. That, too, was perfectly natural. Anytime a qualified behind-thinker leaves his house to pack a car full of boxes during a rain storm, the inevitable result is always imprisonment. "Honest, Officer. I never planned to even leave the yard. No, thanks. I'll forego the phone call. It could only make matters worse."

The nicest thing about being a certified behind-thinker is that the sooner you get to thinking behind, the longer you have to start thinking ahead. When I saw those blue lights flashing in the rain behind me, my brain shifted from fifth gear to reverse. While this drastic brain maneuver does cause a feeling akin to an ice-cream headache, it is not as bad as it sounds. My brain's transmission was just put in backwards, if you know what I mean. In fact, my brain working in reverse produces essentially the same result as your brain does while functioning normally. So, I made the shift and started thinking ahead.

There was no use trying to outrun the cop. I was driving two cars. There was no sense trying to explain the situation to the officer. I barely believed it myself. For some reason, I looked at my wrists and noticed that I still had packing tape wrapped around my cuffs. It was a bit frayed, and the ends were dangling, but it was otherwise intact. I suddenly had an idea.

The Escort was still on the other side of the lay-over road, cruising right beside me. We were just beginning to head up a hill. I let off the accelerator in the Jeep, let the Escort drift ahead of me, and then slipped in behind it. The unmanned Escort fought gravity halfway up the hill, but it was a losing battle. I managed to keep the Jeep right behind the Escort as it cruised uphill, and as soon as I saw it quit moving forward, I jerked the Jeep into neutral and engaged the emergency brake. The Jeep jolted to a stop. I felt the Escort bump into the front of the now stopped Jeep. I lay down on the seat of the Jeep just as the police car raced up behind us.

The officer came rushing up to the driver's side of the Jeep, pistol and flashlight drawn. I lay very still, with my hands up.

He said, "You have the right to remain silent. . . ."

I said, "Quick. Before he gets away. Stop him!" I pointed to the Escort.

The officer dashed up to the Escort, gun ready, shouting, "Halt! Halt!"

After a minute, he came back to me. This officer was plenty agitated; he was wet, scared, and shivering. He still had his gun out, so I lay perfectly still in the Jeep. He said, "What in the blue blazes is going on here?"

I swallowed hard, and started in with a story that was half behind-thinking, part thinking ahead, and maybe a third lateral thinking. I held up my taped wrists and said, "It was awful, Sir. I heard a noise in my backyard, went out to see what was going on, and there was this guy loading up a bunch of stuff from our storage shed into the back of his car. I started to yell at the guy and jumped in his car to try and shut it off, but he knocked me on the head, taped up my wrists (I held up the evidence for the officer to see) took my car keys out of my pocket, got in my Jeep, hooked it up to his own car, and shot out of my yard. He robbed my shed, assaulted me, kidnapped me, and then stole my Jeep." I paused to catch my breath, and then I said, "I got my hands free just as we started up this hill, and jerked the emergency brake up. I guess that stopped him. Did you catch him?"

The officer, looking sort of astounded, shook his head, and then said, "Ah, no. He must have jumped out of the car and run away. We'll, um, we'll check the registration on that car, and track him down that way."

I thought back, which is radically different than behind-thinking, to Paula's good old uncle and his unregistered cars. I tried not to smile. Paula would not be sad when I told her that I decided to give up mechanical endeavors, or when I told her that I had gotten rid of the Escort. I was thinking that soon enough I could put all this behind me.

The Ultra-Secret Advanced Armadillo Reconnaissance Unit

As I sat in the dark Mississippi night, I could hear the din and clatter of an advancing armadillo. I had been pondering the idea of the armadillo in general. They are nasty little devils that look like a cross between an ankylosaurus and an opossum. Armadillos are not overly intelligent, they are self-centered, they have no respect for personal property, and they sort of stink. I would not be surprised to find out that they are some sort of prototype of the human race. Perhaps, since they do not pollute their environment or engage in politics, they are a more advanced model. Nevertheless, they were the enemy, and I was on a seek-and-destroy mission.

I was at my in-laws' house in Mississippi. For the past decade or so, my in-laws have spent considerable time, effort, and money landscaping their yard. They have done most of the work themselves and are rather proud, rightfully so, of their gardens, lawn, and flower beds. During this same period of time, the local armadillos have joined forces in rooting, digging up, and generally vandalizing the yard. When my father-in-law had the yard sodded, for example, the armadillos came into the yard, dug their noses under the sheets of fresh sod and, quite literally, rolled the sheets of sod up like carpet, in order to reach the earth and worms beneath. Had the armadillos then rolled the sod back into place my in-laws might have forgiven them. But armadillos are as likely to clean up after themselves as frat boys. Thus, war was declared.

It was a tricky war to wage though. Armadillos are nocturnal, and even then they don't get really active until long after the local TV station has signed off with the *Star Spangled Banner*. My in-laws, on the other hand, are in no way nocturnal. By ten o'clock they are generally dozing on the couch or in bed. It was, therefore, a war of inconvenience. The armadillos refused to come out during the day to be shot at, and my in-laws were not going to spend every night of the week out in the yard. It would have been a stalemate except that I'm not sure the armadillos were even aware that they were under siege. They spent the wee hours of the night advancing their lines and digging-in without even realizing the tactical value of their movements. They were like an idiot savant S.E.A.L. team of Napoleons—with exoskeletons.

To combat the onslaught, my father-in-law, a retired tank commander, considered contacting some old National Guard buddies and securing a box of land mines. But my mother-in-law wisely pointed out that if they put land mines in the yard, they would have to put a minesweeping device on the front of the riding lawn mower. Moreover, she argued that if an armadillo ever happened onto a mine, the explosion would probably gouge a much bigger crater in the lawn than ten armadillos could dig in a month. Chagrined, my father-in-law cleaned his shotgun and started drinking a pot of strong coffee at 8:30 every evening. He still fell asleep at ten, but the coffee increased his nocturnal trips to the bathroom threefold. Each time he got up in the night, he took a flashlight and the shotgun out to the back porch, and every few nights another member of the ultra-secret Advanced Armadillo Reconnaissance Unit would be listed as Missing In Action.

It was a war of attrition if ever there was one, and with the armadillos losing as many as three of their number a month, they couldn't possibly hope to last under the assault for more than one, or maybe two hundred million more years. On the other hand, my in-laws were not interested in eradicating the whole world's population of armadillos, but rather just those that lived within striking distance of their yard. So the conflict was manageable, and not likely to escalate.

The armadillos, however, found allies in a cult of suicidal opossums bent on yard domination, and a skunk built like a battleship equipped with long-range spraying capabilities. With only one shotgun, and a finite number of trips to the bathroom per night, my father-in-law could not possibly stem the tide, so he called in a specialist. Me.

Specialist might be too strong a word. I have not been formally trained in anti-varmint operations, nor I am especially adept at negotiating peaceful resolutions to armed conflicts. What qualified me as a specialist, in my father-in-law's eyes, is my keen ability to stay awake past ten o'clock. I love staying up late and I readily agreed to take on the task of armadillo liquidator while I was visiting.

I don't know if armadillos are crammed full of courage or just plain bad at being prey, but they are not hard to hunt. First of all, they are noisy. They sound like canned goods falling from the top shelf of a superstore. On top of that, they do not seem to posses the tricks of the trade that keep other game alive. A deer, for example, spends a good part of the day listening. Rabbits practice camouflage pretty well, mice flee from the slightest hint of trouble, and even an opossum will play dead. But not the armadillo. I believe the armadillo species suffers from a genetic syndrome that inhibits their abilities to see, smell, and reason. They will walk into a crowd of gun-toting yard guards without a second thought. They do not readily scamper off at the first hint of trouble and they will not avoid a source of cigar smoke, even if the source is sitting in a lawn chair at two in the morning with a shotgun across its lap. Talking doesn't stop them from waddling about, and, as I found out while doing a complicated scientific experiment, neither does head back, wide open-mouthed snoring.

So, there I was, in my in-law's backyard, shrouded in a thick haze of mosquitoes who were laying waste to the surface of my body. For a moment I thought maybe the armadillos had induced the mosquitoes over to their side, but then I realized that mosquitoes are an enemy unto their own. They are like looters: always present in times of battle, to the detriment of both sides. And then came the familiar din and clatter of the armadillo.

I had devastated their ranks. In five days I had earned the chance to paint the silhouettes of five armadillos on the armrest of my lawn chair. I was an Ace. And here came another. He approached in the usual way, a hurried rattle, making a beeline for a moist spot in the yard. His rattling took on a rhythm all its own and I imagined him singing to himself, "Worms and grubs, worms and grubs, gonna root me up some worms and grubs."

I could see his outline in the moonlit yard, and I took aim. My finger was so swollen from the mosquito bites that it barely fit in the trigger guard. I pulled the trigger and . . . nothing happened. I wedged my swollen finger further under the trigger guard and tried to fire again. Nothing.

There are many mistakes that a man can make while operating a firearm, but the safest mistake, by far, that a man can make is to just plain forget to load the thing. No one, and nothing, except the man's pride, is wounded by an unloaded gun going off.

The armadillo, unperturbed by my shouts and curses, rattled on toward the bug-rich ground. I sat back down, heavily, and watched mosquitoes vaporize as they tapped into my boiling blood. The next day I was unceremoniously discharged from yard guard duty and sent home.

The war, however, rages on. Well, maybe not *rages*, let's say rattles. The war rattles slowly on, one trip to the john at a time.

Vanity PL8

When Skeeter got his pickup truck, about two days after he turned sixteen, he was the happiest boy in all of Halfdollar. It was a used, green Ford F150. There were only 37,000 miles on the odometer, but the odometer was in the glove box and mechanically disassociated from any other part of the vehicle. The truck shone in the sun like dusty jade and smelled like fermented pecan pie, inside and out. The seat was patched in several places where it had been torn over the years, and torn in several more places where it hadn't been patched. The truck had been four-wheel drive, but the last owner hadn't wanted to spend the money to get the left rear wheel repaired after a little accident he'd had, and so while the truck ran fine, it was only three-wheel drive. And, there was something wrong with third gear, so you had to rev up real good in second gear and then leapfrog it into fourth. Finally, the truck had huge off-road tires, with enough clearance to pass over a sleeping mule without waking it, should one be so inclined.

"Ain't she a beaut?" Skeeter asked me.

I just nodded and started to get in. I grabbed the door and the doorframe, put my left foot on the floor mat, and heaved myself up toward the cab. The floor mat sank beneath my left foot like a trapdoor, and I was soon sitting astride the doorjamb, right leg outside the truck, left leg through the floor of the truck.

"Oh yeah," Skeet said, "I forgot to tell you that there's a hole in the floor, underneath the floor mat. Be careful about that."

I climbed in the cab, finally, and placed my feet shoulder width apart, on either side of the gaping hole beneath me.

"It ain't much of a hole," Skeet commented.

"No," I agreed, "but if it was in the roof of the truck, instead of the floor, you'd have yourself a convertible."

"No way," he said, "that hole wouldn't amount to more than a sunroof."

We pulled out of the driveway and headed toward Main Street. I reached over to roll down the window in my door, grabbed the crank, took a quarter turn, and the window just went "thunk," and vanished deep within the door frame. "Oops," I said.

"Darn it," Skeet said, "now look what you've done."

It was shaping up to be a real beaut of a truck.

About four weeks later, Skeeter's license plate arrived. "Is that a vanity plate?" I asked.

"No," he said, "I asked for one, but Dad wouldn't let me get one."

"Hum," I said. "It sure looks like that plate was specially made, with just you in mind." The plate read '1D10T.'"

Skeet held the plate in his hands and studied it. "I don't get it," he said, puzzled.

"Never mind," I said.

Skeet screwed the new plate onto his truck and looked at it again. "1D10T." He tilted his head, squinted, and fumed, "Oh man, that ain't right! That just ain't right! It looks like it says 'IDIOT.'"

"More like a humility plate, than a vanity plate," I commented.

"I can hear people now," he lamented. "'Here comes Skeet in the Idiot Truck.'"

"Looks like rain," I said, changing the subject.

"Rain?" he asked, "No, it looks like 'idiot'."

"The sky," I said, pointing to the sky. "The sky looks like it might rain."

"Sure enough. We'd better put some plastic over your window."

We got a roll of duct tape and some clear plastic, then we sealed up the gaping passenger side window as best we could. As we drove along, the plastic slapped back and forth in the wind and made an awful racket, but it kept out the cold and rain well enough.

We were going over to Philippi to pick up some lumber from the hardware store for Skeet's dad. We were taking the back way, so that we would come in above town. There was a college up there, and it was Friday afternoon, so we hoped we might catch a glimpse of some of the college girls. On the way over to Philippi, it started to rain, and then snow. Huge, heavy snowflakes fell like sod. Skeet decelerated on the now treacherous road and turned on the windshield wipers. They were ponderously slow, but incredibly powerful.

"The guy that sold me this truck said he put snow wipers on her," Skeet said proudly.

"Snow wipers?" I asked.

"Yep, just look at them."

As the wipers made their slow strokes I noticed that they were indeed not normal wipers. In fact, they looked like the scoops off of toy bulldozers. "Are those 'dozer blades?" I asked in astonishment.

"Yep. The guy said he bought four old Tonka 'dozers, took off the blades, welded two pair of them together, coated the edges with rubber, and attached them to the wiper mounts. They work wonders on snow though, that's for sure."

"Except that they are so slow," I added.

Just then we hit a clear patch of road and Skeet sped up. Low and behold, so did the wipers. Skeet looked at me, then out the window, and sped up some more. So did the wipers.

"Holy cow!" Skeet said. "The standard wiper motor must not have had enough torque to move those blades, so he must have hooked them right up to the truck engine. The faster we go, the faster they go!"

"Now that," I said, "is just good thinking!"

After some experimentation we settled on a speed that was slow enough to keep us on the icy road, but fast enough to keep the windshield clear. We made it to the hill above Philippi without incident, cruised the college campus, and then headed downhill, into town. It was snowing harder than ever now, and we had to slow down to almost a crawl to get down the mountain. Skeet was in first gear with the engine barely turning the wheels. By the time we were halfway down the hill, the wipers were moving so slowly that tundra was beginning to form on Skeet's windshield. Skeet, very cautiously, applied the brake, slid in the clutch, and shifted out of first and into neutral. With both hands firmly on the steering wheel, he turned to me and said, "Hold on, I've got to clear the windshield." Then he revved the engine hard. The wipers jumped into action, dug into the tundra on the windshield, and cleared it in no time, throwing great heaps of snow left and right, off the truck.

Glad to have the windshield clear again, Skeet relaxed his foot on the gas pedal and his grip on the wheel. We both looked out the freshly cleared windshield, and then screamed in horror. Crossing the road, not twenty yards in front of us, was a little old lady, pushing her little old dog in a baby carriage. She was bundled up tight against the weather, and not paying the least bit of attention to the traffic. She was coming across the left-hand lane, and headed right into our lane. We couldn't possibly stop on the icy road before we hit her, so there was nothing for Skeet to do but throw the truck in gear and gun the engine. The motor was still running hard from clearing the windshield so Skeet, in a fit, tried to jam the truck into third gear. The gears barked and the truck jumped. Remembering there was no third gear in his truck, Skeet jumped her into fifth, laying off the clutch and onto the gas in a furious but fluid movement. The truck shot past the old lady just as she made it to the double line, leaving her and her dog dazed, but unhurt.

The windshield wipers were wiping back and forth so vigorously that the rubber on the blades began to peel away. Before Skeet could let off the gas the unprotected, metal, bulldozer blades were gouging into the glass, digging deeper and deeper. By this time we were almost at the bottom of the mountain, and thus at the intersection, and doing about seventy-five miles an hour. Through the flying glass of the windshield we could see that an eighteen-wheeler was jack-knifed in the intersection. Skeet made a real hard left toward town, sliding and fishtailing like mad. We missed the truck by inches, and flew into the covered bridge on one wheel. We slammed into the inside wall of the covered bridge just as the windshield wipers finished cutting through the windshield. Now there were two metal blades flinging themselves back and forth in front of our faces, like straight razors. I ducked the blade on my side, and when I did, I shifted my feet, planting all of my weight firmly on the floor mat. Of course, the only thing under the floor mat was the hole in the floorboard, and it was through that hole that I fell, straight toward the road below. It was as unceremonious a way to exit a vehicle as I had ever dreamed of. I did, however, manage to grab the gearshift before I fell all of the way through the void.

When I looked to see what Skeet was up to, I saw the windshield wiper on his side grab hold of his scarf. With a resounding "WMPFTTTT," Skeet was pulled even more unceremoniously out of the vehicle. He went right out the windshield, or at least, right out the hole where the windshield used to be. Skeet managed to lock his knees around the steering wheel. I can't say what was happening to the rest of him since I could not see the rest of him. I could, however, hear him shouting something. I soon made out words. He was saying, yelling really, "RED LIGHT! RED LIGHT!"

There were, at that time, only two traffic lights in all of Barbour County, West Virginia. One was in Belington, some fifteen miles up the road. The other was on Main Street in Philippi, some fifteen yards up the road.

With my feet hanging out of the floor of the truck, one hand on the ripping seat, and the other on the gear shift, there was very little I could do about the fact that we were headed toward a red light, but I felt it was my duty to give something a try.

Holding fast to the gearshift, I pulled myself up through the floor until I could get my right hand on the brake pedal. My feet were still hanging out of the hole in the floor, so I could get very little purchase. Still and all, I managed to push hard on the brake pedal. The truck began to buck a bit, and also to slow.

"Don't stall it!" Skeet yelled. "If the engine quits I'll lose the power steering."

I hadn't realized it, but he was, in fact, steering with his knees.

I've never been very good at driving vehicles with standard transmissions. It continues to perplex me why an engineer would design a system that required a person to manipulate three pedals (gas, brake, and clutch) with only two feet (right and left). And then you still had to hold the steering wheel and work the stick shift. Well, I didn't have to worry about holding the steering wheel, at least I had that going for me. I am not a person who can easily and skillfully administer the use of more than one limb at a time. Anyway, Skeet was still screaming and we were still careening toward the intersection.

After a long few seconds, I managed to get my legs into the truck, and brace my feet on the door panel. I was rolled over, my back on the floor of the truck, looking up at the bottom of the dashboard. I couldn't see the various pedals, but I soon found them with my hands. I pushed hard on both the break and the clutch with my hands while biting the gearshift and trying to downshift using my jaw. It is not as simple as it sounds. The truck made an awful sound. The gears ground, engine surged, and I felt the back end sliding to the left.

"What are you doing?" Skeet yelled. "Don't give it gas. Stop us!"

"Gas?" I asked myself. And then it hit me. I was flying upside down, so to speak. I had my right and left all muddled. Instead of pressing the brake and clutch, I had pressed the gas and brake. No wonder I couldn't shift gears. Quickly correcting my hands, and biting harder into the gearshift, I managed to get us in first gear. The truck slid to a stop. I saw Skeet's knees relax. I let off the clutch and the truck jerked as the engine stalled. I got up slowly.

Skeet lay across the hood, ice matted in his hair. People on the sidewalk stared at us. The light changed to green and, after a second, the guy behind us honked his horn. The bystanders chuckled at that. Skeet got off the hood and into the driver's seat. "I hope," he said, "that you didn't mess up the clutch."

I couldn't think of anything to say to that, but when he shifted into second gear, the stick shift broke off in his hand. I just spit out some metal slivers, and laughed.

That spring I got my own truck, and everything was right with the world until my license plate arrived. "M-Zero-R-Zero-N."

Avant Garden

People garden for many reasons: for leisure, for hobby, for health, some even for sustenance. My dad, on the other hand, gardens for the same reason that the United States and the USSR kept right on building nuclear weapons, going far beyond logic and means should have dictated.

Gardening is Dad's deterrent to a massive, full-blown, vegetable assault. You see, my father is a small town pastor in West Virginia, and thus he is a cultural target for excess produce. For a solid century-and-a-half pastors were paid with food and goods instead of cash. Parishioners simply gave their religious leaders all the extra long-necked squash and zucchini that came out of their gardens.

The tradition hasn't changed all that much, and a pastor just can't say "No" to the little gray-haired ladies who so lovingly grow all that long necked-squash and zucchini. And the only thing Dad hates more than long necked-squash is zucchini. He was once forced to accept a squash and zucchini pie. He took it home, threw it in the trash can, and wrote a thank-you note which read, "Thank you for the pie. I can assure you, a pie like that doesn't last long in a house like this."

Because Dad cannot stomach all that squash, or risk his position by refusal, he practices a bit of small town détente. Dad plows up a good sized, rectangular garden in the yard, where it is readily seen by all passing cars. Then he plants five rows of corn, four rows of sunflowers, and one package of squash and zucchini. And that's it. That's the sum total of Dad's gardening for the year. After that, he just lets it go, grow what will. No fertilizing, no watering, no weeding. It is a very Darwinian approach to horticulture.

After a month or so, Dad's garden gets, well, unruly. To some, Dad is seen as sort of a garden slumlord, letting all the delinquent plants and weeds sprout up, intermingle, and cross-pollinate. Your average tulip or marigold just would not feel safe in Dad's garden after dark. But to Dad, it is beautiful. Stately sunflowers standing by Queen Anne's lace, corn stalks giving shade to dandelions, and squash vines growing willy-nilly and hither-tither. Our neighbor, a tidy man, once told Dad, "Your garden reminds me of my brother's garden. Now mind you, my brother is inclined to be lazy." But Dad just smiles. He calls it his Avant Garden.

And best of all, true to his squash and zucchini non-proliferation strategy, when the little old ladies approach Dad after church on Sundays with big bags of yellow and green gourds, he can assuage his guilt, and spare their feelings, by saying, in all honesty, "No thanks, I grow my own. And I've got more than I could possibly eat."

Something in the Water

I was stunned, dumbstruck. My mother's power of perception never failed to both amaze and shock me. She stood by the kitchen sink, drying a tall glass with a terry cloth dishtowel. She laid the glass in the drying rack, glanced at me, pulled another dripping glass from the dishwater, and said it again:"You've sure been acting weird since you got home from camp. There must be something in the water up there."

How could she possibly know? Had someone ratted us out? It was uncanny how she could have intimate knowledge of events that happened a hundred miles away, on a moonless night, with all the standard penalties of double-secret-hope-to-die-stick-a-needle-in-my-eye promises of loyalty having been given by all parties present. How could a mother know? And then there was the way she let on that she knew. Mom would never just come out and say, "I know all about Lake Suer, at Scout camp." (Lake Suer was named for Perrier Suer, a French Canadian explorer and real estate developer in our area.) No, no, she had to be coy and say, "There must be something in the water up there." But how could she know? How?

It had been a simple mistake, an oversight really, a lapse of good judgment, a speed bump on the road of reason. No malice had been intended, there had been no premeditation, no conjuring, no taking advantage of a dithering old scoutmaster who was given to irascible fits over day-old dirty dishes, bottle caps, gum wrappers, rusty nails, and minor conflagrations.

Mr. Van Crinkle, our scoutmaster, had been, as far as we could tell, an assistant scoutmaster under Lord Robert Baden-Powell, and he always told us that he had "fought under Roosevelt in the War!" But we were never sure which Roosevelt, or in what capacity Van Crinkle had served. There was serious speculation that Van Crinkle had served directly under Teddy Roosevelt, as Roosevelt's personal mule, and had only later morphed into a bipedal, hominoid scoutmaster.

Van Crinkle was shriveled, mean, bitter, and as irreligious as the brig on a pirate ship. He was, I believe, the author of most four-letter words and the coiner of the better phrases involving four letter words and your mother. For some reason, he spoke with a crisp German accent when he had his dentures out, but then perfect Confederate American when he had his dentures in.

Van Crinkle was an oddly vain man. I honestly believe that he did not care, at all, what folks thought about him, or how he dressed, or how well he groomed himself, or how often he bathed. Nevertheless, he was deeply upset that he was bald, and so he wore a toupee everywhere he went. My guess is that he figured that if he didn't have hair people might mistake him for a buzzard, which is ridiculous because he was noticeably shorter than your average buzzard.

To top it all off, Van Crinkle was always mad, but you could tell just how enraged he was, at any given moment, by his accent. His accent, after all, was relevant to the time of day. He got up at what we called the "Crack of Doom." Just after the sun came up, Van Crinkle would hop out of bed, slip his dentures in, his toupee on, and then he would shout us out of bed with his Southern twang in place and intact. If he was up in the morning and shouting, that meant that he was as happy as he could be; which wasn't very happy, but was better than nothing. Van Crinkle was at the age where he was always pleased to have woken up one more time. But if he was speaking with the German accent, well, God help you.

If he was doing his German accent, especially if he was changing his 'W's into 'V's and his 'TH's in 'Z's, that meant that he didn't have any teeth in at all, and that meant he had been awakened from a deep sleep. And if Van Crinkle was awakened from a deep, bald, toothless sleep, especially by teenage Boy Scouts who were supposed to be observing the lights-out regulation, well, just trust me, it was bad news to hear Van Crinkle sounding off like a constipated Kaiser. "Vhy are you boys valking around making enough noise to vake za dead?"

Don't get me wrong though, we thought the guy was great. My dad was the local preacher and Skeeter's dad was a mathematician. These are not occupations given to producing campfire stories that start, "So there we were, the @#!* enemy all 'round us, and us drunk as #@!$ from the hooch we stole from when we robbed the bar the night before, and so Rudolph, he's dead now, killed by his third wife's mother over custody rights to two mules and goldfish, but anyway, Rudolph says to me, 'Well, @#$! Crinkle, are we gonna $#@! *%&$ fight or are we gonna #$%@ !#$% you stupid $%^*-of-a-!@#$. . . '" But all love and admiration aside, Van Crinkle was still mean, and on the third day of camp we concluded that we would have to teach him a lesson.

The third day of summer camp started out like the two before had. Van Crinkle sprang from his tent, teeth in place, and toupee adhered with glue. However, rather than just dressing us down and making us pick up gum wrappers and bottle tops scattered about the campsite, he announced, "Boys, I've noticed that there are nails in the picnic tables that we eat on." He looked at us sternly, waiting for us to contradict him. When we did not, he nodded and went on. "Those nails are rusted and brown. That is intolerable, unsanitary, and gross. You boys will spend your day rectifying that disgusting situation. You will disassemble the picnic tables, pull the nails, sand them, and then polish them until they shine like stars. Now get to work!" With that, he strode off down the path.

"No way," said Skeet.

We all agreed. It was a stupid idea, but we were used to Van Crinkle's stupid ideas and, like good Scouts, we tried to be prepared for anything he might think up. We held a quick powwow and then sent Jimmy running down to the Trading Post where he bought two bottles of silver model paint and eight paintbrushes. We deftly painted the top of each nail gleaming silver. It took only twenty minutes to do the job, but we'd decided we'd definitely had enough of Van Crinkle's little camp improvement chores. So we came up with "The Plan."

For the rest of the day we went about business as usual, moving from merit badge classes, to canoe safety classes, to fishing, to meals, and finally to bed, all the while avoiding Van Crinkle.

Long after everyone was supposed to be in bed, Skeet and I peered into Van Crinkle's tent. He was snoring softly, his toupee-less head tilted back and his toothless mouth gaping. As usual, his teeth were on the bedside stand and his toupee was laying on a newspaper under his cot. Skeet and I woke the rest of the troop and the eight of us snuck into the dining hall.

We made our way though the dark building to where the old mountain lion stood in the corner. Every Scout in the Buckskin Council knew that lion, and everyone just called him Gene. Gene was a huge mountain lion that had begun his life in the wild, but in his youth he got mixed up with a bad crowd. Gene got hooked on human food and rubbish. He became a garbage junkie and ended up scavenging trash dumps. Late one night he was caught, convicted, and sentenced to life in the local zoo. Incarceration didn't really bother Gene too much though. He died reformed, happy, and peacefully, of old age and circus peanuts.

Since Gene was a mountain lion he didn't leave a will, or indicate what he wanted done with his remains. Since he had outlived all of his kin, no one objected when it was decided that Gene was to be stuffed, standing upright, with his eyes glaring and his teeth flashing. Eventually, Gene found his way to the Scout camp and was now serving a stint in what must be mountain lion Hell. He was forced to watch and smell all that food which was just beyond his stuffed paws. It was sad really. Here was this old garbage junkie forced to stand in the midst of his wildest dreams and yet be eternally denied his fix. The old beast looked fierce, even if he was wearing sunglasses, a bandana, a baseball cap, and three or four pounds of spilled food in his fur.

We wrestled Gene onto a handcart, lashed him on with rope, and wheeled him back toward our campsite. The first thing I noticed when I pushed Gene out into the fresh night air was that he smelled like every meal that had ever been cooked in the dining hall. He emitted an odor of scrambled eggs, bacon, tacos, meatloaf and sloppy joes which was quickly caught by the breeze, and drifted off into the forest like food perfume. Before long we noticed raccoons and skunks creeping behind us and sniffing the air, intrigued, but not overly willing to attack a lion, no matter how dead he was or how delicious he smelled. Little did we know that we had just unleashed a scavenger's Pied Piper on the world.

Our campsite was situated halfway down a steep hill. At the top of the hill was the dining hall, at the bottom of the hill was Lake Suer. Just before reentering the campsite we paused to reconnoiter. I shined my flashlight in a quick arc to see if all was still in our site, and to check that no other mischief was afoot. I was amazed, and a little distressed, when I noticed the eyes of dozens of small creatures burning hungrily back at me from just inside the tree line.

We quietly wheeled Gene directly in front of Van Crinkle's tent so that the outstretched forearms of the mountain lion were inside the flaps of our cranky leader's tent. We were all standing around Gene, in front of the tent, arguing quietly about the best way to position Gene, and laughing softly over the thought of Van Crinkle's expression when he woke up in the morning and saw the mountain lion just entering his tent. And then we heard a slight rustling sound coming from inside the tent. It sounded like fingernails tapping on the wooden floor of the tent, the same sound a hand searching for a toupee on a wooden floor might make. We left old Gene where he was, and we backed away into the night. I had just slipped into my tent when a flashlight beam burst forth from Van Crinkle's tent. The light hit Gene right between the eyes. I heard Van Crinkle scream, "Great Scott! Zere is a mountain lion in za tent! Vere is my hair!" His feet thudded on the floor and then Van Crinkle sprang from the tent with surprising agility, hitting Gene square in the chest, and wrapping the beast up tight.

As I have explained, our campsite was on a slope, a

hill really, which descended steadily and ended at Lake Suer. As I have further explained, Gene was strapped to a pushcart and was thus on wheels. It doesn't take much imagination to figure out what happened in the ensuing few moments. Van Crinkle, holding the lion tight, and screaming accented obscenities, rolled down the hill and into the lake. There was a distinct splash, and then he was sloshing back up the hill muttering more accented obscenities.

The unobvious portion of the account is much more exciting and was later related to us by Skeet. When we heard Van Crinkle moving around, Skeeter had ducked behind Van Crinkle's tent and was peering through the rear tent flaps as the action took place.

Skeet had seen Van Crinkle's head roll over, his arms twitch, and then the old man sit up. He put his arm to the floor and began searching for the heap of fur that was his toupee, all the while keeping his eyes on the blurry figure in the door of his tent. The tapping sound that we heard was indeed not Van Crinkle's fingernails tapping the floor, but rather a skunk that was doing a little recon on the food-scented lion, on behalf of the rest of the rodent army hidden in the woods. Just as Van Crinkle dropped his hand to the floor to start blindly searching for his toupee, his fingers lit on the skunk's back. Van Crinkle, as Skeet explained it, never looked down. He just plunked the skunk onto his baldness, leapt from his bed, and rushed old Gene. The skunk, not at all understanding what was going on, but realizing that he was now flying through the air at teeth level with the food perfumed mountain lion, was too scared to spray. Instead, he just dug all four feet into Van Crinkle's scalp.

The lion started to roll backwards, Van Crinkle holding to Gene's chest, the skunk holding tight to Van Crinkle's head. The other skunks, opossums, and raccoons in the woods, upon seeing the valor of the skunk on Van Crinkle's head, were rallied into action. Hundreds of furry creatures attracted by the strong scent wafting from Gene's culinarily saturated hide burst from the woods and gave chase. Some of those pouring out of the woods ran right through Van Crinkle's tent. Being an honorable bunch of creatures, they were loathe to leave any of their wounded or dead on the field of battle, and so when one raccoon passing through Van Crinkle's tent spied the toupee lying on the floor, he naturally thought it was a fallen brother and hefted the lifeless form onto his back.

Van Crinkle was brave and fought like a tiger. He wrapped his legs around Gene and started punching the lion in the ribs. The hits thudded up the valley like someone chopping oak logs with a twelve-pound axe. And then Van Crinkle tried to bite Gene. His toothless mouth posed little threat to the already dead, but rather quick, mountain lion. Gene merely continued to roll backwards down the hill, drawing ever closer to the lake. When Van Crinkle bit Gene without the benefit of his teeth, he got a mouthful of fur. He drew his head back sharply, tasted the fur in his mouth, sniffed the lion, saw the sunglasses and bandanna, and slowly realized he was fighting Gene on wheels. Van Crinkle, concluding that he was in no great danger, relaxed his grip, his adrenaline output abruptly halted, and his nerves once again began transmitting information other than "KILL KILL" to his brain.

The closest, and thus first heard, nerves to speak to Van Crinkle were those nerves being assaulted by the skunk atop his head. For the life of him, Van Crinkle couldn't figure out why his toupee hurt so bad. Feeling the claws in his skull, Van Crinkle reached up to check his toupee. With a mighty jerk he brought the skunk off his head and in front of his eyes. When you realize that you are holding a skunk inches from your mouth and nose, your body does funny things. Van Crinkle tensed all over again and raised the skunk as if to throw it. Gene was still rolling downhill, ever closer to Lake Suer.

The pack of berserk woodland creatures behind Gene, Van Crinkle, and the brave skunk charged on, unaware that the lion was stuffed with fluff and not eggs, bacon, tacos, meatloaf and sloppy joes. The raccoon with Van Crinkle's toupee on his shoulders led the pack, the toupee flapping the breeze like a hairy cape.

Just as Van Crinkle was about to toss the skunk, the raccoon with the toupee cape left the ground and sprang for Gene, the skunk, and Van Crinkle. Just as the raccoon vaulted for the trio, the trail ended in the lake. Gene's wheels hit a rock and Gene, Van Crinkle, and the skunk flew out over the placid surface of Lake Suer clinging together like melted jelly beans fused by the summer sun in the backseat of a '67 Mustang. The raccoon with the toupee cape sailed out behind them.

On the shore there was a massive, multi-creature pile up as hundreds of skunks, raccoons and opossums screeched to a halt and crashed into each other. Skunk glands went off like air bags on impact and the air was filled with a vile stench.

Out over the lake the four warriors and the toupee achieved their maximum velocity, began to slow, and thus started to drop toward the water. There was a tremendous splash, the sound of which rushed over the lake's surface, through the skunk stink, over the animal wreck on the shore, up the path and into our tents. We scouts received the sweet song of the splash as we lay on our cots. The splash song was caught in the folds of our canvas tents like a spider web in the breeze, and the melody hung there teasing our eardrums and emotions for a long, rapturous moment. The sweet reverb of the splash faded into a gurgle, and then was crushed beneath a loud, Germanic tirade of soaked curses and drenched obscenities.

Suffering with the urge to laugh, I and the other scouts lay in our bunks as Van Crinkle sloshed into camp. He went straight to his tent, without a word.

When Gene turned up missing the next morning there was a general ruckus and hubbub among the camp leaders as to where Gene was and what should be done about his theft. We worried about Van Crinkle letting on, but he never said a word about the ordeal. He just went bald for the last few days of camp. We scouts swore secrecy and never had to pick up a bottle cap or paint a nail again.

When I got home I was as happy as I could be. Occasionally I would just laugh out loud when I thought of the whole affair, but I never spoke a word. Never told a soul. And yet my mom knew. She stood by the kitchen sink, drying a tall glass with a terry cloth dishtowel. She laid the glass in the drying rack, glanced at me, pulled another dripping glass from the dishwater, and said it again: "You've sure been acting weird since you got home from camp. There must be something in the water up there."

How did she know that out in there in the water, far below the weeds and lily pads of Lake Suer, resting in the mud, as the white bellies of the fish passed slowly overhead, lay an ugly toupee and mountain lion named Gene who was, at last, washed clean of his food scent and freed from his prison, the cafeteria that was his lion Hell, to at last rot away and leave the world for good. All of that lay under the water, that, and a touch of Van Crinkle's pride, and a dash of his crankiness.

Fat Bats

My neighbor's wife was a gift from God for anyone who might one day be compelled to break the tenth commandment. That is to say, if my neighbor's wife was the last neighbor's wife on earth, I would not, under any circumstances, covet her. She was built like a snowman melting in the sun. She only wore shirts that exposed her midriff, and she only wore cut-off shorts. She held a Ph.D. from Harvard in Multi-Cultural, Matriarchal, Mother God, Pantheistic, Liberation Theology. She had a collection of tattoos which she had spent many years gathering. Some reflected her time spent in the South Pacific with the Merchant Marines, some her time spent in the African jungles as a Peace Corps volunteer. One was from her sorority days at a southern college. One was to show her solidarity with women unjustly imprisoned in the Northwest Territory. Others were merely decorative. Many of the tattoos were on her belly. She also had an ever present cigarette in her mouth. She never touched it with her hands, it just hung in her mouth, usually stuck to her upper lip. The cigarette moved with her upper lip as she talked, and often added ashes to anything she said. Her name was Mindi.

Her husband, Geoff, was a scholar also. He held a Ph.D. in Masculine Representations of the Deity in Post-

Biblical, Neo-Classic Literature of the Perka-Perka Island Peoples. He weighed nearly as much as a beehive in May. He drank, on average, enough beer each day to float the Lusitania.

Mindi and Geoff had only their odd scholarship and their love of grilled food in common. They grilled every meal, every day, except on Christmas Day. On Christmas they deep-fried a goose, just to maintain their redneck status. All rednecks, and trust me I know, must deep-fry something, at least once a year.

Last spring the cicadas came to town. They sat in trees and chirped away, ceaselessly. Big, fat bugs filling the air with their songs, their hard bodies flying about in great flocks, colliding with everything from people to cars to houses, and their dead bodies littering the ground. It made it tough to be outside. Any person mowing a lawn was pelted by a constant wave of shattered cicada parts. Mowing a cicada-littered lawn was like a contest on *Fear Factor*. Every evening at dusk there was a dense cloud of cicadas in the sky as far as the eye could see, which wasn't far, because of the dense cloud of cicadas in the sky.

It was fun, however, to sit in a protected shelter during the evenings and watch the bats come in and sweep the sky for cicadas. The bats were getting fat. They hardly even needed their echolocation. A bat could just open his mouth and fly through the sky. Cicadas would flow down his throat whole. Mindi and Geoff would sit on their porch, grilling, and argue about the sentient value of the bat versus the cicada. Which had the right to eat the other, which had the right to exist unhunted, which had the right to spawn, fly, rest, procreate, and continue? All the while, they grilled cows, chickens, pigs, and lambs, over charcoal.

Fat bats are fun to watch fly because as their bodies get larger, their wings don't. It looks like the wings shrink. Imagine a groundhog trying to fly with hummingbird wings. And, as the bat takes on weight, it loses its keen maneuverability. We've all seen slick, slender bats darting through the sky, diving, pulling out of dives, spinning, performing precise loops. It's like watching the Blue Angels. But, when you rapidly increase the weight of a bat, without also increasing the wingspan, well, fat bats lose their ability to pull out of dives as quickly. It is not nice to say, but it is funny to see a bat the size of a groundhog nosedive into the yard. Nature provides a satisfying "FFWUMP" sound when the bat hits. If you are lucky you can even hear the bat grunt. If you are luckier still, you can hear Geoff and Mindi wail over the senseless brutality of nature, as spare ribs sizzle on their grill.

And then, having ceased to be airborne, the fat bat is unable to get up enough power to take off again. They hit the ground, right themselves, shake it off, and then flap their wings once, confidently, the way they would in any normal circumstance in order to get airborne. Nothing happens. Perplexed, they flap harder. Still nothing. Next, the fat bat will try a running take off. They waddle across the yard as fast as they can, flapping like mad, trying to build up enough ground speed to get the air flowing over their wings. The thing is, a bat's wings are very extensive and encompass a huge portion of the bat's body. Their wings, just so you know, are actually their arms and hands. If you look closely at a bat's wings you will see the elongated bones of the bat's fingers. The wings start at the shoulders of the bat, extend down the arm, over the elbow, to the thumb, all way across to the pinky, and from there, down the side of the body, over the legs, and into the tail. They are not built to run and flap their wings at the same time. Imagine trying to run and flap your arms with a short rope tied from your wrist to you ankle. Bats are simply not designed for a running take off. But then bats are not designed to eat so many cicadas that they weigh as much as a Thanksgiving turkey.

One of several things happens once the bat starts running. It either runs so far that it loses enough weight to take off again, or, exhausted, it looks for a place to rest. Bats, of course, rest by hanging upside down in trees or belfries. But a fat bat cannot get to one of these locations. It was not uncommon during the cicada days to come out and find bats, dozens of gorged bats, hanging from the undercarriage of your truck. Occasionally, you would see vehicles speeding down the highway, bats hanging tenaciously to whatever they could grab. Some bats would launch from this position, using the speed of the moving car to assist their take off. It was not unknown for a flock of bats to rise from beneath a speeding truck, much to the consternation of the driver directly behind said truck.

Other bats, too fat to get their feet above their heads and hang, would just curl up in a hole, or sleep right where they fell. Some bats walked all the way to the local church, down on Main Street in Halfdollar. They forced open the church doors, found the entrance to the bell tower, and took the stairs.

Fat, running bats also attracted the attention of creatures not normally interested in bats. Neither *Wild Kingdom* nor *National Geographic* ever had any footage so interesting as a stray cat fighting a fat bat. Dogs too. Dogs would chase the bats for hours. The bats just didn't know what to do. They aren't ground creatures. They couldn't figure out how to outwit a dog. Plus, bats legs were not created for long haul transportation. Have you ever seen a toddler, having recently learned to walk, suddenly try to run? Well, put useless flapping wings on him, and you've got a fat, running, grounded bat.

Buck-dog, my super hound, thinks he likes to eat

bats. To this day he will stand in the yard at dusk and leap, straight up, to try and grab bats out of the sky. But, as far as I know, he has never eaten a bat. It happened like this.

I was in my backyard, watching the whole fat bat show, and chatting with my neighbor, Geoff, across the yard, who was getting his grill fired up for a little cookout. Buck was curled up at my feet. Suddenly, a gigantic bat fell out of the sky, not ten yards from me. It grunted, drawing the attention of Buck. Buck looked up, saw the strange creature, and lit out to investigate. The bat, thoroughly confused, was sending radar waves out in every direction. He quickly detected the fast approaching form headed his way. At first, the gluttonous bat opened his mouth, obviously thinking Buck was a giant cicada. Then Buck barked.

The bat shot across the yard at as fast a waddle as he could, rocking back and forth on his spindly little legs, and flapping like mad. Buck was closing in fast. The bat came to the edge of our yard. Our yard ends in a steep incline as it drops toward the Pocatalico River. Just as Buck snapped his teeth, the bat hit the drop-off. He somersaulted once or twice, hit a rock, and bounced twelve feet into the air. Buck leapt upwards at the bat just as the bat spread his wings and lifted like an obese hang-glider into the sky. The bat had just enough momentum to get airborne, but he was skimming the ground. Buck over shot him by eight feet. The bat continued to follow the contour of the sloping ground and then glided out over the river, skimming the surface. Buck ran along the shore, pacing the distressed bat.

Bats were not the only creatures getting their fill of the cicadas. Trout, martins, spiders, and bullfrogs were also feasting and fattening. The bat was just regaining some control of his flight facilities as he glided over the weeds on the edge of the river. He was finally beginning to ascend. Going into a shallow right hand turn, he seemed intent on cruising just over Buck's head. The bat had about twelve inches of altitude when he over-flew the weeds and crested the bank of the river. Just then, the long, pink tongue of a frog shot out of the brush and stuck to the belly of the bat. The bat was on maximum power though, trying to escape Buck, and so he just kept on flying. The frog, about the size of a cantaloupe, rose out of the weeds and hung from the flying bat like a bat hangs from the undercarriage of a speeding truck. The bat, undaunted, continued to climb. But, just as bats are not used to being on the ground, so frogs are not used to being in the air. But this was one tenacious frog. He started to reel his tongue in, and pretty soon, he was belly-kissing that fat bat.

As the bat climbed to about twelve feet, with Buck-dog still following the action, the frog did an amazing thing. He swallowed that fat bat in mid air. It was not a particularly wise move, but then we don't expect frogs to be smart. He swallowed the whole bat, except the wings, which stuck out both sides of the frog's mouth, and were still flapping furiously. The frog had, quite literally, bit off more than he could chew, and the bat, so completely incapable of understanding what was happening, just kept on flapping. The thing is though, the fat bat was having enough trouble keeping its own great weight airborne. Furthermore, and despite what you have heard elsewhere, bats are unaccustomed to flying inside of frogs. So, the bat quit flapping its wings just as it crossed over the border of my neighbors' yard. Frogs cannot fly. The huge amphibian began tumbling out of the sky.

It was getting almost too dark to see by this point but, as I said, my neighbor was starting a fire in his grill so there was a bit of light, just enough to see the descending frog was headed right for the table next to my neighbors' grill. The frog hit the table hard, landing right in the middle of a plate containing the two whole chickens Geoff was getting ready to cook. One whole chicken flew into the air and was swallowed, mid-flight, by Buck-dog. Buck came into our yard as fat as a bat-eating frog. Geoff, who had stepped into the house to get his fourteenth or fifteenth beer, missed all of this. He came out of the house, checked the grill, and then, without really looking, picked up what he thought were the two whole chickens on the plate next to the grill. The cold skin of a dead frog, with a bat inside, would, I figure, feel a lot like the cold skin of a dead chicken to a drunk guy, in the dark. Geoff flopped the two "birds" onto the grill, shut the lid on the grill, downed his beer, and walked back inside.

I know that the right thing to do would have been to tell my neighbor. But, on the other hand, I was greatly interested in how all of this would come to an end. There are certain questions in life, certain quintessential lines of inquiry which, once opened, must be answered for your life to have continued meaning. Questions like: Is there a God? Why am I here? And of course, what happens if you have a frog, stuffed with a bat, stuffed with cicadas, and introduce into this equation the element of fire?

Remember those urban legends about the lady who accidentally put her cat in the microwave? Or better yet, remember making popcorn before the advent of the microwave? Remember those things popcorn used to come in? Those Jiffy-Pop things? It was like a pie tin, with a coat hanger for a handle, and the whole thing was covered with a thin sheet of aluminum foil. You put it right on the eye of the stove and the foil would rise as the corn popped? And, if you let it go too long the foil would break open and popcorn would fill the kitchen? Well, whole cicadas locked in the belly of a bat, locked in the belly of a frog, put on the grill, react a lot like popcorn kernels in a Jiffy-Pop rig. I heard the fire crackling, then I heard a lot of popping, and then the lid of the grill started to rise on its hinge like a vampire's coffin.

My neighbor, Geoff, stepped out onto his back porch, beer in hand, and looked at the grill. He turned his head to get a better perspective. He flipped his hand in front of his face to clear away the oncoming bugs, and then stepped toward the grill. Popped cicadas were coming out of the grill like crumpled wads of paper toward a substitute teacher. He took a sip of his beer, stopped, scratched his head, took another tentative step forward, and then called quietly, in a very unsure voice, "Honey?" And then, regaining confidence, "Honey. HONEY. HONNNNEY! What in tarnation did you stuff them chickens with? I told you to quit watchin' TV just before you cooked. I told you to stop readin' them fancy magazines. HONNNNNNNNEY!"

My neighbor's wife, Mindi, came out the back door. Mindi said, "I didn't stuff them birds with nuthin.' What are you talkin' abo. . ." And then she saw the lid of the grill fly backwards and a wave of puffed cicadas swallow her husband. "OH FATHER IN HEAVEN!" she cried. "It's like that movie we watched about them alien bugs. Run for your life!" And she was gone, over the railing, into her VW bus, and down the driveway, fat bats bouncing from the undercarriage in all directions. Geoff had vanished into the fluff of the popped cicadas.

I walked over to his yard. He offered me a cicada. "Folks eat popcorn shrimp," he said. I shrugged my shoulders. Turns out that popcorn cicada ain't that bad, though I'd rather have a corn kernel caught in my teeth than a cicada wing.

Now, just to make sure the People for the Ethical

Treatment of Animals don't get in a fuss, I assure you, no animals were hurt during the writing of this story. The frog, it turns out, was suffering from a heart condition and, as the autopsy later revealed, would not have lived much longer anyway. The cicadas were dead almost as soon as the bat swallowed them. And the bat, well, the bat was protected by the fat insulating the interior of the frog, so the frog's fat batting saved the bat from the fall, the grill, and the fire. The bat, having had his dinner toasted out of him, left his fat in the fire, and emerged from the flames as right and true as a Louisville slugger.

The cicadas eventually disappeared, the bats resumed normal eating habits, Mindi soon came home, Buck-dog is still waiting for a fat bat to plop out of the sky, and Geoff, well, Geoff has quit drinking and uses a flashlight to thoroughly inspect anything he puts on the grill.

Naaman and the Hiccups

Adapted from II Kings: 5

Naaman hiccupped from dawn to dawn, day after miserable day. This is bad enough if you are just a regular guy trying to do your job, but Naaman was a general. He led behind-the-lines attacks and secret operations involving stealth and silence. It is hard to be stealthful when every few seconds an awful "HI-UPPPP!" escapes from your throat. It is not only embarrassing, but also deadly. It also does not instill respect from your men.

Let us pause here for a historical statement, and a statement of explanation. Naaman, commander of the army of the king of Aram, was a great man, as far as his King was concerned, because the Lord had given victory to Aram through Naaman. That is to say, Ben-Hadad II, king of the Arameans, liked Naaman because Naaman was a good general. This would have been sometime after the eighteenth year of the reign of Jeshoshaphat, king of Judah, or, as we say these days, in the 850s, before the common era. The Arameans and the people of Israel were technically at peace, but there was still bad blood, and the occasional border skirmish, between them. So, they did not like each other.

The thing is though, Naaman had leprosy. Leprosy, as you know, is the general biblical term for any of a number of skin diseases, most of which have been eradicated in this day and age, in this country. We are, thankfully, unfamiliar with leprosy. So, for the sake of this story, we will redact, re-edit, and mistranslate. Let's say that Naaman was greatly afflicted with the hiccups. We have all been afflicted with this particular woe from time to time, and Naaman had it bad.

Naaman had in his house a servant girl, captured from the Israelites, who served his wife. This servant girl served her mistress with diligence and devotion, and she knew how hard it was for her mistress to put up with Naaman's hiccups. It was, for example, hard for Naaman to get smooth with his wife, to sweet talk her, to set the mood, if you see what I'm saying. Imagine, Naaman comes home after a long campaign, the candles are lit, there's a nice bottle of wine on the table, fresh flowers in a vase, newly plundered jewelry on Mrs. Naaman's neck, fingers, ears, toes. Naaman says, "Hey baby, HI-UPPP!, I missed you. HI-UPPPP!" He takes a sip of wine, and HI-UPPPS it all over her new dress. Not cool. Not to mention that it was difficult to get a good night's sleep lying next to a man HI-UPPPPing every thirty seconds.

The servant girl, seeing the stress the hiccups were causing, said, "It's a shame you aren't in Samaria. There's a prophet there who could cure Naaman's hiccups, and then you could go on with your lives."

Naaman hiccupped, then ran to his king and said, "My servant girl has said HI-UPPP that there is a prophet in Samaria HI-UPPP who can cure my HI-UPPP hiccups!"

"Really?" said the king. "I'll write their king a letter and see if we can get you in to see this prophet. I'm not sure your health plan covers out-of-the-country prophetic visits, but perhaps we can get one of our prophets to refer you to him. That way you'll get your 80-20 payment, but I'm not sure if it will go toward your deductible."

"HI-UPPPP" was all Naaman could say.

And so, Naaman set off with his aides and adjuncts to visit the Samarian prophet. When they got to the king of Israel's palace, Naaman showed King Joram the letter and gave him, by way of a gift, ten silver talents, 6,000 gold shekels, and ten festal garments. It is not that the king of Israel needed all that gold, or those festal garments, but, well, he was a bit of a clotheshorse. And, you must remember that Israel and Aram were essentially at war. If you are going to send your top general over to your enemies' prophet to be healed, it is best to grease the path with a bit of gold and garments. It just makes good sense. Nowadays, of course, the king of Aram would have sent the king of Israel three pounds of Starbucks gourmet coffee, one golden disc worth 10,000 free minutes on AOL, and an eighty-dollar gift certificate to The Gap, or maybe L.L. Bean.

The letter read:

Dear Jo,
This is my general Naaman. He has a bad case of the hiccups. I understand that you have a prophet over there who is linked up pretty tight with God and who can cure the hiccups. Please accept these gifts as payment for your guy healing my guy.
                              All the best,
                              Ben II

"Holy Cow!" exclaimed King Joram. Seeing the gifts and reading the letter from Ben-Hadad II, Joram rent his garments (the ones he was wearing, not the new ones). "Does your king think that gold, silver, and festal garments can buy the power of God to heal a man? Does your king know nothing of faith and obedience?

Is this some kind of a trick? Your king sends you here, my prophet is supposed to heal you, and if he can't, then your King takes it as a slight on my part and has an excuse to attack me all over again. This is bad, bad stuff."

Naaman said, "HI-UPPP Please sir, it is no trick."

Now, Elisha, the prophet in question, heard of the king's outrage, and the rending of his garments, and sent word asking, "Why have you torn up your clothes? Tell Naaman to come to me and I will heal him, and he will know that there is a prophet of God in Israel."

Naaman, naturally, went to see Elisha at Elisha's home. Naaman stopped outside Elisha's door, and Elisha, not bothering to come out to meet him, yelled through the door, "Go and wash in the Jordan seven times and your hiccups will be cured."

Now, this made Naaman exceedingly angry. He had, after all, come a great distance, at great expense, to see Elisha, and Elisha wouldn't even answer the door, just yelled through it. Naaman fumed, kicked up some dirt, and generally made a fool of himself. "Dip in the Jordan seven times?" He exclaimed. HI-UPPPP! "We have rivers in our land which are far better than the Jordan. I can dip in those!" HI-UPPPP! "What I want is a cure. Something complicated, something difficult. Only that sort of thing will cure the hiccups. That man didn't even come out to see me. He could have laid hands on me, had a long sermon and an altar call, said a spell, anything." Spent from his tirade, Naaman turned and headed home.

One of his servants, however, rushed up and said, "General Naaman, if Elisha had come out and said, 'Swallow seven spoonfuls of sugar as fast as you can,' would you have done it?"

Naaman hiccupped and nodded his head in answer.

"If he had told you to put a paper bag on your head,

hold your breath for twenty minutes and spell your mother's maiden name backwards, would you have done it?"

Naaman hiccupped an affirmative.

"Had he commanded you to hop on one foot through a prairie dog town while whistling Dixie, or to stand on your head while reciting the pledge of allegiance, you would have done all or any of that, right?"

"I certainly, HI-UPPP, would have," said Naaman. "A man needs a complicated cure for the hiccups. It is a complicated condition which calls for a well thought-out, obscure, and sometimes humiliating cure. This prophet is a quack and his God is a ninny." HI-UPPP.

"Well," the servant said, "maybe that is the point. Maybe it is we who want a complicated solution to our problems, while God is often willing to offer a simple solution, if we will just be obedient to God's word. We've come all this way, why not just jump in the river?"

HI-UPPPP." OK, might as well." And Naaman went and dipped in the river, just as the man of the Word of God had instructed, and when he arose the seventh time, his hiccups were gone, and his life was restored to its pre-hiccup status.

Artist's Renderings

"Lieutenant Stepp," the Colonel was asking, "do you know why I have had to call you into my office yet again?" The Colonel scratched the top of his head with the bottom of his West Point ring.

"Sir," Lieutenant Stepp started, raising his hands and shrugging his shoulders.

"Can it." the Colonel shouted. "You've screwed up so much that you could probably list a dozen reasons why you think I have called you in here, but I don't want to know what the heck you have been up to. If you start confessing, I'll have a mountain of paperwork. I'll just cut to the quick."

"Thank you, Sir," Stepp said, relieved.

"Shut-up."

"Yes, Sir."

"Why the ROTC recruiters accepted your application in the first place, I will never know. God must hate the U.S. Army."

Stepp smiled at that.

"Don't say a thing, don't smile. Just stand there and listen to my tirade."

"Yes, Sir."

"How you lived through the war, I will never know. You're so bone-headed that dogs must follow you around. But here's the thing. Did you play poker last night?"

"Yes, Sir."

"With those VIPS from Japan?"

"Yes, Sir."

"And did you win?"

"Yes, Sir."

"How much?"

"Sir?"

"Don't be daft. How much money did you win?"

"Well."

"Answer the question Stepp. It's not hard."

"Well, Sir," Stepp cleared his throat, "I won about twelve grand."

"Twelve grand! Lord love us all! You, a sorry ROTC lieutenant from the motor pool won twelve thousand dollars from a visiting General! Do you have any idea how bad that makes me look? I don't even know why you would be playing with those big-wigs. . . ."

"They asked me to, Sir," Stepp inserted.

"Shut up. Now look, you've made us look bad, real bad. My boss has gotten wind of this. That visiting general is piqued and ashamed. He lost a lot of face, losing to a ninny of an officer like yourself."

"Sir," Stepp pleaded, "they asked me to play."

"For the love of God! Shut up! Now listen, this is causing a stink. That general complained to our general, said he didn't know you were playing for keeps, thought it was a game for fun. . . ."

"Sir, that's crazy," Stepp tried.

The Colonel leaned back in his chair. "Crazy or not, it is causing trouble way up and down the line. Now, here's the thing Stepp. If you give that money back, and apologize, we can all get on with our lives and sweep this unfortunate incident under the rug." The Colonel made a gesture with his hands of lifting a rug and brushing dust under it.

"No." Stepp said, sliding out of his position of attention.

"No what, Stepp," asked the Colonel, going rigid and coming forward in his chair.

"No, I won't give the money back, and I surely won't apologize. That general is a big boy. If he didn't want to lose, he shouldn't have played," Stepp answered, sliding back into a more formal stance.

"Look, Stepp," the Colonel said coldly, "I can't make you give that money back. But I can tell you, in no uncertain terms, that if you value your military career you will see to it that that money gets back to that VIP general." The Colonel slammed his fist down on his desk, knocking the mug he kept his pencils in to the floor, where it shattered.

"I don't, Sir," Stepp said loudly.

The Colonel was coming slowly out of his chair, his hands flat on his desk, his forearms twitching. "Don't what, Stepp?" he asked.

"I don't value my military career."

The Colonel fell back into his seat, his face gone plum. He started to shake. Stepp stepped backwards, making for the door. He walked backwards until he hit the door with his rear. Stepp found the knob, turned it, and slipped out of the Colonel's office as the Colonel sat shivering with anger in his chair.

Outside, Stepp lit a cigarette and thought to himself, "Three months. That's all I have left. I survived a year in the jungle, I can survive three months in Maryland." He strode across the base to his quarters.

"Hey, Slim," Stepp said in greeting to his roommate, who was sitting at a desk reading.

"Hey, Stepp. What did the Colonel want?" Slim asked.

"Wanted me to give that money back to that foreign general."

"Are you going to give it back?" Slim asked.

"Not a chance. I won it fair and square," Stepp replied, lying down on his bunk.

"Colonel Pine is going to kill you," Slim said, turning back to his book.

"I got three months left. He can do what he wants." Stepp shut his eyes and drifted to sleep.

•••••

Two days later, on Friday, Stepp, Slim, and ten other junior officers were gathered in the command conference room, waiting on the Colonel for their weekly staff meeting. The conference room was in a World War Two era building, built when the base needed cheap structures set up fast. The building had not been meant to stand for longer than ten years; now it was decades old. The walls were buckling; the ceiling was stained. On the back wall hung a United States flag, on the other walls were maps of the world. There were no windows. In the center of the room sat an oak table, polished like a mirror all along its fourteen-foot surface. Around the table were folding chairs.

Slim leaned back in his chair and scanned the room. He said, "There are thirty-six of us that are supposed to be at these mandatory weekly meetings. How do so many guys get out it?"

"Lots of ways," Stepp answered. "These meetings are for crap and everybody knows it. You can call in sick if need be, or just get your Captain to write you an excuse. You'll learn."

The Colonel came through the door and all twelve lieutenants jumped to attention, saluting.

"Take your seats men," the Colonel ordered. "First thing on the agenda this week," the Colonel looked at Stepp, "junior officers are from this day forward prohibited from playing games of chance with visiting dignitaries."

A snicker floated through the room.

Colonel Pine cleared his throat and continued, "Next item. It's the end of the budget year and the base is low on funds. Each of you will be provided with a list of ways your company can cut back. You are to share these lists with your direct superiors and discuss ways to save money in your units."

"Maybe," came a voice from the group, "Stepp will loan the Army the money to get through."

The Colonel ignored the comment and went on. "Stepp," he said, "I have a special mission for you."

Stepp looked up and saw the Colonel smile.

Colonel Pine said, "I was thinking that the yard in front of my office lacks authority. It needs something to give it a little panache. I want you to think of ways of improving my office lawn."

"Yes, Sir," replied Stepp.

"Fine, give me a report next week on what you come up with."

The meeting drifted on, nothing critical being discussed or solved, and then the lieutenants were dismissed.

Walking toward the mess hall, Slim asked, "Stepp? What are going to do about the Colonel's office yard?

"Nothing," Stepp answered.

"Nothing?"

"Yep, nothing. Tomorrow I am going on special duty, a training mission in the swamps, I'll be gone for two weeks, two staff meetings. By the time I get back, the good Colonel will have either added his own panache to his lawn, or forgotten the whole thing," Stepp said.

"And if he hasn't?" Slim pressed.

"Slim," Stepp put a hand on the other man's shoulder, "you've only been in the Army six months. I've been in nearly four years. Just trust me, Colonel Pine will forget his panache. And even if he doesn't, when I get back I'll have ten weeks left in the Army. If it comes down to it, I'll drop my pants and crap in the Colonel's lawn. If that ain't panache, I don't know what is."

•••••

Two weeks later, a collection of lieutenants were once more gathered with Stepp in the conference room. The meeting was coming to an end when the Colonel said, "Stepp, what have you come up with for my lawn?"

Stepp, sitting up straight and dropping the tooth-pick he had been cleaning his nails with, said calmly, "Sir, as you know, I was in the swamps for the last two weeks. I was thus, unfortunately, unable to put in the time needed to spruce up your lawn."

"Well," Colonel Pine said with a smile, "I've come up with an idea. I want you to go over to that state park next door and Federalize me a boulder."

Stepp squinted, "A boulder, Sir?"

"Yes Lieutenant, a boulder. A nice big one."

After the Colonel left the room Slim asked, "What now, Stepp?"

"Same plan as before. Nothing. Ten weeks."

"That's a long time," Slim said doubtfully.

"Slim," Stepp said, getting up, "watch and learn. I can put the Army off for ten weeks. What I won't do is get myself arrested by some state park cop for stealing a boulder."

"Arrested?" Slim asked. "If you went to get a boulder and somebody asked what you were doing, you could just say the Colonel told you to get one for him."

"And then," Stepp said, "the cops would call the Colonel. The Colonel would deny all knowledge and send the MPs to come drag my butt to the base slammer. No thanks."

"Why not just ask the state park people for a boulder?" Slim suggested.

"Because, Slim, I'm not going to do it at all. I don't care about the Colonel and his stupid boulder."

•••••

Word was traveling around the base about the Colonel and his boulder. Odds were being given, bets taken, on the eventual outcome. Most surprising, however, was that attendance at the weekly meetings was on the rise. Twenty of the officers required to be at the next meeting were there, only sixteen had shirked the meeting. They wanted to see what Stepp would do next, but Stepp was among the shirkers.

When the meeting was over, Stepp found the conscientious Slim. "So?" Stepp asked.

"Nothing," Slim responded. "Colonel Pine looked around the room, saw you weren't there, and never said a thing about the rock. But you have eight Fridays to go before you are out of the Army. You can't ditch them all."

"I only have seven meetings. My last day in this Army is a Thursday," Stepp recounted. "But I don't plan to skip them. I have a plan." He winked at Slim, stuffed his hands in his pockets, and walked off across the base.

•••••

The Colonel went through all the regular routine at the next meeting, closed his folder, and then, looking around the crowded room, said, "I'm glad to see so many of you in attendance. This week only eight of you are missing. I am especially glad to see that Stepp has decided to join us." Colonel Pine looked at Stepp. "Where's my boulder?"

"Sir," Stepp shouted, leaping from his chair and jumping to attention, "I was unable to secure the use of a backhoe and truck. I was told I had improper authorization to take such machines off base, Sir." He sat down.

"Very good, Lieutenant," Pine said, "I'll speak to Major Coldwell in the motor pool and explain the matter to him. You are all dismissed."

Slim leaned over and said, "Six meetings to go. Most guys are betting against you."

Stepp smiled. "How 'bout you Slim?"

"I've got a month's pay that says that the Colonel will get a headstone before he gets a boulder.

Stepp smacked Slim's shoulder and laughed. Stepp walked the length of the glossy oak conference table, dragging his hand across the smooth surface as he left the meeting room. He walked toward the motor pool and Slim saw Stepp hand Major Coldwell an envelope.

•••••

"Sir," reported Stepp at the end of what was now known as Boulder Meeting T Minus 5. "Major Coldwell informed me that he had received your clearance for the required trucks and materials, but the backhoe was out of commission and won't be up and running until various requisitioned parts are delivered and installed."

•••••

Thirty-three lieutenants, the Colonel, and his aide, were crammed around the conference table for Boulder Meeting T Minus Four. The time came for Stepp to deliver his report. "Colonel, with all do respect, I happened to be reading base regulations and I noticed that the regs clearly state that, for safety reasons, any non-mobile, non-structural, non-foliage article on base over eight inches high must be painted yellow or orange so that it does not pose a health hazard. By nature, Sir, boulders are over eight inches high."

Colonel Pine frowned deeply. His brow creased. "Stepp," he said finally, "you get me that boulder, make it at least twenty-four inches high, put it in my office lawn, and let me worry about the safety regulations. Do you understand me?"

"Yes, Sir," snapped Stepp.

• • • • •

T Minus Three. "Sir, the backhoe operators were indisposed. One in the infirmary, two at training."

• • • • •

T Minus Two. "Stepp," the Colonel was shouting into the faces of all thirty-six lieutenants seated around the table, "if you don't have some positive results concerning my boulder next week, I'm transferring you to Alaska!"

• • • • •

There were the thirty-six regulars, plus a smattering of other officers who found a reason to attend the meeting all stuffed into the conference room. Stepp opened the door and slipped into the room about half-way through the proceedings. He made his way to the far end of the room and leaned against the wall, his hands in his pockets. His expression gave nothing away. Energy filled the room, all eyes going from the Colonel to Stepp. The Colonel kept his face in his papers, droning through the exhaustive routine of giving his underlings things to do. At last he looked up. "Stepp," he said coldly.

Stepp moved to the edge of the table, the men around it giving way. He stood directly across the table from the Colonel. The table's surface reflected the overhead lights and the faces of the men sitting around it. Stepp pulled his right hand from his pocket. His hand was closed around something, and he shook the contents like dice. "Colonel," he said, "I am pleased to announce that I have conducted a careful examination of all the boulders at the state park." He paused, looking straight at the Colonel. Stepp shook his hand at table level, and then flung something across the tabletop. As the small objects clattered across the smooth oak surface toward the Colonel, Stepp said, "And I have had an artist render some scale models of the boulders I thought you would find most attractive." The small objects slid to a stop against the Colonel's chest, which was pressed against the far end of the table. The Colonel looked down and saw that the objects were a handful's worth of gravel at the same instant that the rest of the officers recognized the objects. In the brief silence that followed, Stepp said, "If you will choose one, I'll go and fetch it, Sir."

The Fall of Babble-On

Author's Warning. This story contains many, varied, and very bad puns. Reader discretion is advised for those with Pun Tolerance Disorder, small children, expectant mothers, those with heart conditions, and the sober.

Early one Sunday morning I was taking a walk in the woods near my house when I began to hear a sound like trumpets, coming from over the mountaintop. The trumpeting had a church-like quality and, it being Sunday morning, I thought perhaps some congregation had decided to take its services outdoors. Intrigued, I turned toward the sound and headed uphill. Not wishing to disturb the service, I flattened myself on the hilltop and slowly inched my way toward the edge of the rise. I was amazed at what I saw when I looked over the hill, and a voice inside my head said, "Write this down."

Down below me, on the river's edge, there was indeed a church service of some sort going on, but it was not humans worshiping. It was animals instead. I watched closely for some time trying to figure out what was going on. Hundreds of different species were gathered around a central figure who was leading the group in a song. There were skunks, beavers, bears, cows, birds, mice, rats, raccoons, bugs, and dogs. I did notice, however, that there were no Dalmatians. I guess it was a Non-Dalmatianal congregation. They also had a candelabra set up, bearing seven burning candles.

The creature preacher finished his sermon to the faithful flock by saying, "I know your works, your toil, and your patient endurance, and how you cannot bear evil men." Behind the creature preacher were seven seals with the trumpets I had heard, a small rodent who must have been a chipmonk, wearing a brown robe, and quite a few praying mantises. Behind the seven seals stood seven horses dressed in colored choir robes. The horse chorus began singing as the ushers began taking up the collection. The ushers were all huskies, with shining coats and bright blue eyes. The head usher, I was surprised to see, was in a fact a man wearing a parka and leaning on a sled. I quickly surmised that he was the usher musher. As the ushers came forward with the tithes, an ox stepped forward and, appropriately, led the group in the doxology. "Praise God all creatures here below," he sang, "except Dalmatians and buffalo." When the offering was taken, a door opened in a tree and out stepped a rainbow trout. The rainbow trout sat down in a throne and around him sat twenty-four adders. Around the trout's throne there sat a lion, the ox doxologist, the usher musher, and an eagle. The eagle must have been Catholic, because everyone addressed him as Cardinal Eagle.

The Cardinal, who was actually an eagle, rose and asked who had come to be baptized, and from the congregation stepped a church mouse and a cat. The Cardinal stepped into the stream, said a prayer, and dunked the church mouse beneath the surface. The ushers, the usher musher, the lion, the ox doxologist, the chipmonk, the trout, the adders, the creature preacher, the horse chorus, the seven seals, the praying mantises, and the faithful flock all sang out a joyous prayer. And then the cat stepped into the stream.

The cat stood shaking in the shallow water as Cardinal prayed over him. After the prayer, the Cardinal picked up the cat and dunked him in the water. Again, the ushers, the usher musher, the lion, the ox doxologist, the chipmonk, the trout, the adders, the creature preacher, the horse chorus, the seven seals, the praying mantises, and the faithful flock all sang out a joyous prayer. I didn't know what denomination the animals were, but if they were dunking, they weren't Methodists. Anyway, for a creature that hates water, I felt that the cat had done remarkably well with the procedure. To my surprise, the Cardinal began praying again, and then lifted the cat, and then dunked him again. And again, the ushers, the usher musher, the lion, the ox doxologist, the chipmonk, the trout, the adders, the creature preacher, the horse chorus, the seven seals, the praying mantises, and the faithful flock all sang out a joyous prayer. The cat looked less pleased, but still allowed the baptism. And then it all happened again. And again. Each time, the cat grew more and more agitated. Confused, I thought the matter over and at last, it donned on me. Cats have nine lives, and thus they need to be baptized nine times. Simple theology.

By the sixth dunking, the cat was starting to squirm something fierce. On the seventh he went rigid. On the eighth, he thrust out his claws, and while the Cardinal was praying over the cat in preparation for the final baptism, the cat happened to spot the church mouse sitting atop a rock. The cat looked up at the Cardinal and saw that his eyes were closed. The cat glanced around the congregation and realized that everyone, including the ushers, the usher musher, the lion, the ox doxologist, the chipmonk, the trout, the adders, the creature preacher, the horse chorus, the seven seals, the praying mantises, and all of the faithful flock had their eyes closed. The cat, eight of his souls thoroughly dunked and saved, suddenly decided that he was mightily hungry and that it was better to have eight saved souls and a full belly than it was to have nine salvations and go hungry. Eight parts angel, one part hell-cat, the feline dove for the church mouse.

When the cat dove, he knocked over the candelabra loaded with seven ceremonial candles burning brightly. The candles fell into the pine needles covering the riverbank and the river's edge burst into flame. Hearing the clatter and feeling the heat, the Cardinal, the ushers, the usher musher, the lion, the ox doxologist, the chipmonk, the trout, the adders, the creature preacher, the horse chorus, the seven seals, the praying mantises, and the faithful flock all opened their eyes to the flames, and saw the light. The mostly saved cat landed on the rock where the church mouse had been sitting, but the church mouse was already headed through the crowd and looking to escape.

The seals, seated behind the rainbow trout, panicked and began breaking to the left and right. When the seals broke, the horses in the horse chorus ran from behind them, their white, red, black and tan robes blowing in the breeze as they charged through the crowd of animals, trampling the helpless and overturning the food which the congregation had brought for lunch. And the fire burned up nearly a third of the forest.

The ushers, being dogs, saw it as their duty to chase the hell-cat who was chasing the church mouse. The usher musher followed in close pursuit, followed by the lion, the ox doxologist, the chipmonk, the trout, the adders, the creature preacher and the praying mantises. The Cardinal, who, remember, was actually an eagle, flew strafing runs at the cat's head.

The mouse dodged through the legs of the faithful, and the cat continued his pursuit. The horses of the chorus had calmed a bit and gathered at the far edge of the crowd, attempting to set up a roadblock to stop the cat. Meanwhile, the lion had picked up a pan and was trying to scoop up the cat. While the church mouse ran, the cat fast on his heels, the lion with the pan dashed up and grabbed the cat. The lion put the cat in his pan just as they got to the choir of horses. But, before the lion could thoroughly trap the cat, the cat leapt from the lion's pan into the choir.

The church mouse, the cat, the ushers, the usher musher, the lion, the ox doxologist, the chipmonk, the trout, the adders, the creature preacher, the horse chorus, the seven seals, the praying mantises, and the faithful flock ran faster and faster toward the edge of a nearby ravine. At the edge of the ravine, the church mouse jumped. The cat, with the eight saved souls, and one lost soul, jumped after the church mouse. The ushers, the usher musher, the lion, the ox doxologist, the chipmonk, the trout, the adders, the creature preacher, the horse chorus, the seven seals, the praying mantises, and the faithful flock all stopped short of the edge. The Cardinal swooped down and tried to catch the church mouse, but missed. The church mouse fell all the way down to the stream below, splashing into the deep black waters. The Cardinal corrected his dive and grabbed the cat. Taking the cat to what was believed to be a bottomless pit, the Cardinal dropped the eight parts saved and one part not saved cat into the pit.

The Cardinal, the ushers, the usher musher, the lion, the ox doxologist, the chipmonk, the trout, the adders, the creature preacher, the horse chorus, the seven seals, the praying mantises, and the faithful flock gathered down by the stream to mourn the loss of the church mouse. While they mourned, they noticed a cod swimming upriver with the church mouse on her head. They all smiled in recognition as they waved to the cod, who every one called Grace. Grace had caught the church mouse and delivered him safely home.

So, in the end, most of the cat went to Heaven, the church mouse was saved by Grace the Cod, and the ninth part of the cat, the unsaved soul, spent eternity in Purr-dition.

Quantity 4: Quality 0

The difference between quality and quantity is a multiple of four. Most people are wholly unaware of this statistic and thus I feel obligated to share it with you. This knowledge comes from years of trial and error, with emphasis on the latter. I only had to go to trial once.

Here is an example. Say you are trying to drive a nail in order to affix one board to another. To further illustrate that point, let's just say that you are building an airplane in your garage. Wait, let me explain some more. I'll get back to nails, trust me. When Skeeter and I were eleven years old we learned about the Wright brothers and their flying machines in our American history class. It has never ceased to amaze me what parents object to having their kids taught and what steamy, intoxicating tidbits of information they will happily allow to fill their children's heads. Parents go absolutely insane if you bring up the idea of sex education for eighth-graders, but they don't even blink when the teacher tells her class of impressionable youth that two of America's greatest heroes, in this case the Wright brothers, never graduated from high school.

Suddenly, Skeeter and I had some seriously dangerous information. We broke it down into four parts.

1) The Wright brothers never finished high school; 2) The Wright brothers knew something about bicycles; 3) The Wright brothers built an airplane in their workshop; and 4) The airplane flew. So, while Skeet and I had perhaps missed the whole point of the lecture, thus failing to gain a quality education, we now had four important facts that we could apply to our own lives. We therefore had a quantity education, in four parts. Quality 0: Quantity 4. We quickly applied those four parts and came up with four intriguing similarities we shared with Orville and Wilbur. Like the Wright brothers, 1) We had not finished high school; 2) We knew something about bicycles; 3) We had access to a workshop where we could build a plane, and, 4) because our situation was so similar to the Wright brothers, the plane we built would, obviously, fly. Quantity 4: Quality 0.

So, back to the nails. Reasoning that since the Wright brothers didn't have access to academic works on aeronautics, Skeeter and I figured we didn't need to bone-up on the subject either. If the Wrights could do it from scratch, so could we. In my dad's outbuilding we assembled a pile of lumber, a pair of training wheels, and a ceiling fan. First things first, we laid one twelve-foot board perpendicular atop another, forming what to the untrained eye would have looked like a cross, but to any pilot would have clearly resembled a fuselage and wing structure. Then we began to fasten the two boards together with nails. We considered using screws to hold the wing onto the fuselage because screws are generally stronger than nails, but screws are a lot harder to drive with a hammer than nails. We also figured that since we wanted a fixed wing aircraft, we would need to use more than just one nail. We concluded that we should use four nails to mount the wing. One nail directly in the center of the juncture of the two boards, one nail slightly above the first, one slightly below, and the fourth somewhere to the left. Why? Well, the wood looked softest in those places.

Because we needed four nails, we naturally selected sixteen from my dad's nail collection. Remember, the difference between quality and quantity is always a multiple of four. Skeet and I knew from experience that it generally took four tries to drive one nail straight into a board. The first nail would more than likely spin off into some dark, spider-infested corner of the garage, the second would bend after about six whacks, the third would bend after about ten whacks, and the fourth would go all the way through. Usually, all three of those nails would sink at least partially into the second board and so you had three nails binding the boards together for every one nail needed. So when Skeet had finished driving nails into all four of the spots we had chosen, we had twelve nails at least symbolically holding our wing to the fuselage, instead of just four. Quantity 12: Quality 0.

Once we had the wings securely attached, Skeet and I nailed the ceiling fan blade to the nose of the plane and the training wheels to the bottom of the craft. Because the ceiling fan, now our propeller, was about four feet in diameter, we had to build stilts out of 2x4s so that the training wheels, now our landing gear, kept the propeller off the ground. We did not know much about flying, but we did know that we did not want the propeller hitting the ground. Our plane now had better clearance than most four-wheel drive monster trucks.

The craft was a real beaut. She had a four-foot propeller, a twelve-foot fuselage, and a twelve-foot wingspan. The only problems were that the plane was four feet off the ground and that it leaned to the right. The reason the plane leaned so dramatically was because eight of the twelve-foot wingspan was on the right side of the plane, leaving just four feet on the left side to counterbalance the craft. We considered cutting the right wing down to four feet, but in the end we decided that twelve feet were twelve feet and that it wouldn't make any difference in the air anyhow.

Another thing Skeet and I knew for sure about airplanes was that you had to have an airfoil, you had to consider lift and drag, and we had read somewhere that the airplane had to be able to stand up to tests in a wind tunnel. Well, we didn't have any airfoil, but my mom had lots of aluminum foil in the kitchen and so we wrapped the plane in a double layer of the shiny material. It sparkled in the sun. On the ground, we had to pretty much lift or drag the plane anywhere we wanted it to go, so we figured we were all right in those areas. What we didn't have was a wind tunnel. There was, however, a train tunnel not far from the house, so we lifted and dragged the plane down to the railroad tracks. Once in the tunnel we couldn't think of any tests to give the plane, but it stood up in the tunnel just fine, so we reckoned we were ready to fly. Combining the four things we knew about the Wright brothers with the four things named above that we knew about planes, we knew eight things about the history and science of flight, but nothing really useful. Quantity 8: Quality 0.

Skeet and I wheeled the plane to the top of Pityme Mountain. Pityme was a mountain that offered a nearly vertical road on the way up, but was almost straight down if you were going the other way. Many a child on a bicycle from Halfdollar, West Virginia had gone airborne when they hit the speed bump at the bottom of Pityme Mountain, so we figured we could roll downhill on our airplane, gaining plenty of speed and getting our propeller turning fast enough for lift-off. That way, when we hit the speed bump at the bottom of the mountain, we would just sail off into the wild blue yonder.

On our way up the mountain we discovered that our lopsided wing arrangement was not very effective while the plane was still on the earth. The right wing continually fell and scraped along the road. Skeet pointed out that this might cause trouble during landings and so I ran back to my house and got some more 2x4s, and a pair of old skis. We fastened one ski to each wing using the 2x4s. The skis not only kept the wings off the ground, but made the plane perfect for landing on snow, ice, or water. This was a great boon, since we had no idea where we might land.

Once we reached the top of the mountain we taxied the plane into position, climbed aboard, and picked up our feet. We started to roll. We started to roll faster. It seemed like we might actually get up to take-off speed before we got to the bottom of the mountain except that the tail of the plane refused to come off the ground. The back end of a 2x12 dragging on the asphalt can go a long way toward slowing down an aircraft trying to take off. Sawdust and smoke came off the end of our plane in great plumes. To remedy the situation I motioned Skeet to scoot forward. We inched further and further toward the whirling propeller until Skeet was nearly getting a haircut. Finally the tail of the plane lifted off the ground. For the rest of the way down the mountain, we had to continually shift our weight forward and back to keep the propeller from tipping too close to the ground, and to keep the rear from dropping back to the road.

And then we hit the speed bump. There was a tremendous THUD as the training wheels bounced into the mound of concrete, then there was the distinct sound of wood breaking as the 2x4s attaching the landing gear snapped in two. Following that, the bumping, rocking, and rattling stopped. I felt the wind in my hair, and the mist of the clouds on my cheeks as we passed through them. Later, I would come to realize that what I thought was mist from the clouds was more than likely sweat and tears from Skeeter. He was up front and could see the events unfolding in front of us much more clearly than I. Come to think of it, I hope it was just sweat or tears. Nonetheless, we were flying. I started to count, "One Mississippi, Two Mississippi, Three Mississippi, Four. . ."

I have since heard pilots say that any landing you can walk away from is a good landing. I tend to disagree with that theory. We hit the ground hard. The fiberglass skis attached to the wing tips started to melt as they skidded along the road, and the ceiling fan came off and whipped over our heads like a saw blade. And then we stopped, thanks to a stout tree some kind soul had thoughtfully planted directly in our path. We would have hit the tree much harder except that as the plane slowed, the skis cooled, and the now molten fiberglass turned into a paste that stuck to the road like glue. If we hadn't hit the tree, we would have eventually sunk into the melted fiberglass like dinosaurs into a tar pit.

Later, when I regained my ability to walk, I measured the distance from the speed bump to the first divot the skis had made in the road. We had flown sixty-four feet in four seconds. Later still, when I regained my ability to cipher, I did the math. We had achieved airspeed of sixteen feet per second.

Quantity wise, it was the first time we had ever flown, the furthest we had ever flown, the fastest, and certainly the most fascinating display of airmanship ever witnessed on Rt. 20. Quality wise, well, there was very little about the flight to which you might attribute the word "Quality." So, in the end, the score remains the same. Quantity 4: Quality O.

Stop Sign Man

In the land of Streets and Corners there were many he-
    roes and villains,
But the most heroic of them all,
Was a young boy who stood only three feet tall.

He was small in stature, but possessed of powers un-
    known here-to-for
To any creature that flew, walked or crawled across the
    floor.
He wore a cape, and an armored suit of red;
He carried neither sword nor wand, but a magic stop sign
    instead.

Whenever there was mischief afoot, or a bad guy up to
    an evil design,
Stop Sign Man would arrive in a rush, brandish his octa-
    gon and shout,
"Stop Sign!"
And the evildoer would cease to do his evil doings there
    about.

One day while Stop Sign Man was walking through the
    woods
He heard a sudden scream and squeal.
Rushing up the path he found a family of picnickers be-
    sieged by bears

Trying to steal their meal.
The picnickers were the Macaws, Martin, Martha, Mindy,
    Mike and Neal.
Martin Macaw was warding off the bears with a chair and
    a bicycle wheel
As Stop Sign Man rushed into the breach, and pulled out
    his eight-sided, evil-ending sign of steel.
Shouting"STOP SIGN,"in the faces of the thieving bears.
Stop Sign Man pulled the picnic baskets from the bears'
    claws
And returned them to the hungry and grateful Macaws.
To the bears he said, "Next time remember that it is not
    nice to rob, thieve or cheat.
Now, go home and make a sandwich if you wish to eat."
Shame-faced, the bears beat a hasty retreat.

Later, while walking by the beach,
Stop Sign Man saw a ship anchored just out of reach.
"Ahoy!" came a cry from the ship,
"We're about to have our tea. Won't you come aboard for
    a sip?"
Suspicious of the Jolly Roger flying above the ship's deck,
Stop Sign Man shouted back, "You are pirates, I won't
    risk my neck!"
"Aye," yelled the pirate captain in a kindly voice,
"We are but friendly sailors who dress as pirates by choice.
Have no fear, kind sir, we will not harm thee."
Stop Sign Man flew to the ship, doubting the men, but
    thirsty for tea.
Then as soon as Stop Sign Man landed,
He realized the pirates were naughty, mean, dirty, and
    underhanded.

The quite unfriendly pirates rushed at Stop Sign Man
    with swords rusted by oceanic brine.
Acting quickly, Stop Sign Man bore his four-lettered, scar-

let peacemaker and shouted "STOP SIGN."
He arrested the pirates, and read them their rights from
his handy Miranda card,
Then he promptly turned the bandits over to the local
Coast Guard.

Still thirsty, Stop Sign Man stepped to a small café, to see
what cool drinks they were selling.
When he opened the door he was greeted by harsh, brash,
and ungrateful yelling.
"My lands," he shouted over the din, "What evil is afoot
in this place?"
He heard two children's voices shouting "Gimmie,
Gimmie,""Mine, Mine, Mine."
He saw the children fighting while other patrons tried to
dine.
They grabbed and grunted, never said please, nor thank-
you, burped loudly and were otherwise crude.
"Alas," Stop Sign Man muttered to himself, "It is the en-
emies of all decency, Carmen and Cameron Rude!"
Unstrapping his blazing red, metal manner mender, Stop
Sign Man strode to
The Rude Twins and shouted, "STOP SIGN, PLEASE! Yes,
I mean you!"
Mid-belch, Carmen and Cameron Rude,
Had their manners mended, and changed their impolite
attitude.
"Thank you for saving us from a life coarse, boorish and
rude,"
Said the twins, who no longer suffered from social in-
eptitude.

Leaving the café, Stop Sign Man serenely strolled
Down the lane sipping milk that was ice cold.
He saw three kids flying brightly colored kites at the play-
ground,

But he also heard a darkly sinister sound.
Over the hill, sitting high in their saddles, rode The Three
    Dark Knights Who Most Hated Kites.
Stop Sign Man had fought many battles with these three
    darkly armored marauders
In parks, 'mid fields, on beaches, and twice even in har-
    bors.
They lowered their lances, wielded their swords, unslung
    their slings,
And set about trying to cut the three kites' strings.
"Of all the dirty, rotten, low-down things,"
Shouted Stop Sign Man as he threw his cool drink aside
And he looked all about for his own horse to ride.
Charging straight at the Knights Who Most Hated Kites,
Stop Sign Man unscabbarded his red and white street
    sign of power and might,
Shouting "STOP SIGN!"

But he did not yell at the Knights themselves, but rather
    at the wind.
And as with all things that Stop Sign Man signed, the
    wind could not help but mind.
The kites lingered but a moment in the windless sky,
And then dropped to the ground with a soft sigh.
But the Knights Who Most Hated Kites were in a bind,
For they had aimed their weapons quite high;
Their winded horses whinnied and whined
As the Knights attempted to re-aim their Swords and re-
    wind their slings,
But all three Knights lost their balance before they could
    do any of those things.
They hit the ground and rolled around,
And at last their leader spoke,
"Stop Sign Man, again, you have ruined our plan.
One day we shall capture you and tie you up, like a pig in
    a poke."

Stop Sign Man merely laughed, and said, "Dark Knight,
    that is quite a joke."

As Stop Sign Man was riding his horse over hill and dale,
He heard a girl who had just begun to weep and to wail.
Stop Sign Man then passed an ox-drawn wagon,
Just in time to see Princess Cora almost singed by a fire-
    breathing dragon.
Guiding his horse between the dragon and the distressed
    but royal dame,
Stop Sign Man wielded his rosy polygon of Goodness
    and shouting, "STOP SIGN,"
Shielded Cora from the flame.
The flame, obeying his command, stopped in mid-air.
Stop Sign Man grabbed the frozen flame and with a dash-
    ing flair,
Turned it around and shoved it back down, the dragon's
    reptilian throat with a mighty Shout.
The dragon coughed and wheezed, blowing backwards
    smoke from his snout.
He looked forlornly at Stop Sign Man, and whimpered
    softly,
"If I promise to be nice will you please take the back-
    wards fire out?"
Stop Sign Man seized this unique opportunity,
And made the dragon swear to be good and always do
    his duty.
The dragon agreed to forever uphold the laws of the land
    of Streets and Corners, and by goodness to abide.
And then, surprising both the Princess and Stop Sign
    Man, the dragon became the Man's loyal, magic ride.
Princess Cora and Stop Sign Man climbed upon the
    dragon's scaly back,
And the three of them flew off into the Stop Sign red sun-
    set, nothing did they lack.

A Ride in the Pinpricked Hyphen

In a completely rational world there would, perhaps, be no need for fear. In a rational, ordered cosmos we would not need fear anything because everything would make sense. When a mountain lion suddenly leapt at you from a tree branch you would not be afraid, but rather simply think, "Well, this is all very reasonable. This big cat is hungry and it has a hankering for my perfectly sculpted body in the same way that I often have a hankering for pizza and beer. Surely the pizza and beer feel no fear as I eat them. They understand that it is their lot in the universe to be consumed. Therefore, I can conclude that it is now my lot to be consumed by this springing lion who has a taste for a body, a perfectly sculpted body at that, made primarily out of pizza and beer. I need not fear, but simply submit to this ordered and rational universe, and then I will pass onto the great ordered and rational Beyond."

We all know, however, that there is fear in the world. We may thus conclude that we do not live in a wholly rational world. A clear and evident sign of the unstable, irrational condition of our world is the tiny craft called the kayak. The kayak itself is perhaps not all that far-fetched. I'm sure the inventors of the kayak had a specific, rational intent and use when they came up with the idea, but what is not rational is the way the kayak has been employed in the days following its inception. In case you don't know, people put on skirts, seal themselves into kayaks, don helmets, and go down rivers which God created *specifically* so that people would not try to go down them.

Allow me to point out that any time you engage in an activity that requires you to wear both a skirt and a helmet, you have stepped over the line clearly delineating rational from irrational behavior. Women's roller derby, for example, requires both a helmet and a skirt, and few people will argue the rationality of roller derby. (I will point out, in the interest of not being besieged, that Scottish soldiers wear helmets and KILTS, not skirts. And Scottish soldiers are big, tough, and rational. If they want to wear kilts and helmets, more power to them. If they want to wear kilts and helmets and kayaks, well, that's just not natural.)

Anyway, for a number of years I lived in Fayette County, West Virginia, very near the New River. The portion of the New River which flows through southern West Virginia is perhaps the most famous stretch of the whole river. I would not be surprised to find out that it is the most kayaked stretch of river this side of the Mississippi. If you live close enough to anything for long enough, eventually you get in it, and thus I came to be sitting in the New River wearing a kayak, a skirt, and a helmet. It was totally irrational, but there I was. I knew it was irrational for a number of reasons. For starters, I was a novice kayaker. And for finishers, I was scared stiff. The act of kayaking is not enhanced by stiffness. It is a sport of agility, animation, stretching, leaning, hip-swiveling, and finesse. My fear and physical rigidity were not suited to kayaking, though they would have done me quite nicely had I been in a submarine suffering scrutiny from a SONAR-bearing, depth-charging, destroyer.

Generally, I am a cautious person, not given to careless acts that can easily precipitate horrible deaths, especially my own. So, I had chosen an easy stretch of river to first ply my skilless kayaking abilities. We were miles above the canyon, where the real rapids rage. In fact we were so far above the real rapids that I felt confident that even if I became absolutely wedged in my craft, I would be rescued, or die of starvation while adrift, before being washed into lore. I had plenty of people watching over me; some on shore, some in canoes (a reasonable aquatic vehicle), and still more people in kayaks hovering about. The kayakers were showing off, surfing on the rapids, rolling over this way and that, zipping upstream and down, and otherwise making a spectacle of themselves.

Kayaks are essentially the fighter planes of the river fleet. They approach silently, low to the surface, get in and out of trouble with speed and swiftness, and serve a very specific strategic purpose. The boats are fast, light, lithe, and garishly decorated. The pilots are sturdy, strong, and crammed so full of panache that they simply cannot sink. Canoes, on the other hand, are a little more sober, if a bit more lumbering, and the pilots usually practice more vigilance. But canoes are actually useful. Like a fast bomber, they can serve many functions. Surely they can get in and out of tough spots quickly and efficiently, and deliver a critical payload if need be, but the canoe can also serve a humanitarian function. Like a bomber, they have room to ferry out stranded personnel, or carry in needed equipment like medical supplies, food, and warm blankets. Furthermore, and perhaps most importantly, you can fish from a canoe.

In later days, after the accident I have still not gotten around to telling you about, I tried to fish from a kayak, I even worked hard to convert a kayak into a sort of stealth fishing craft, but it was to no avail. Kayaks serve one and only one purpose, and sadly, that purpose is not fishing.

Now, where was I? Oh yes, I was wearing a skirt and a helmet while facing down a mild set of rapids on the New River as proficient kayakers zipped about me like spawning salmon. It was my wife's kayak. She had bought it at a second hand store for $10, including the skirt, helmet and paddle. We later discovered that the kayak was very old and generally considered a racing craft. It pitched and rolled without hesitation. The mist coming off a rapid and settling too heavily on one side of the kayak would flip it clean over. This particular kayak was so narrow that it had neither a port nor a starboard side, just a middle. It was so thin that it was hard to distinguish the top from the bottom. And the front and rear ends were pointed so severely that you couldn't really say that the boat had a stern or bow. Both ends just sort of drifted off into space like the ends of chalk line drawn on a blackboard to illustrate the infinite nature of the universe. So, I was sitting in a boat that had neither a front nor a back, it was devoid of the utterly useful dimensions which define top and bottom, and the craft wholly lacked a left and a right side. The only thing that could be said that the kayak had for certain was a middle, and there was a hole in the middle, so that I could get into the darn craft. That doesn't leave much. It was like cutting a hyphen out of a document, pushing a pin through the hyphen's middle, and then trying to climb into the hole.

I started above the rapid, and I admit that it was a lot of fun to ride downstream in my hyphen. As I practiced paddling in an eddy, I limbered up, and my courage began to grow. I am a proficient canoeist and so I understand the principles of being on the water, and I can read whitewater fairly well, so I headed back out into the main flow, turned my tiny craft upstream, and began to climb the rapid I had just descended.

I was maybe three strokes up the rapid when my inability to kayak became evident. The kayak began drifting sideways and I swiveled my hips in an effort to correct the drift. As I swiveled, I laid my upper body too far out over the edge of the hyphen, and then I was underwater.

Being underwater in a small rapid is not all that terrifying a happenstance, nor was it a circumstance that I had not lived through before. One simply sticks his feet out in front of himself and swims to the surface as he drifts down stream. No problem. This time though, I was faced with a number of sobering thoughts and realizations, and when you are underwater, stuck as I was, you only have time for a very finite number of thoughts and realizations. First, I realized I wasn't drifting downstream. Second, I realized my head was much closer to the floor of the river than the surface. Next, I realized that I could not flip over. And finally, I realized I was stuck in the kayak. My last thought was, "Oh geez! My mother is going to be mad if I die like this."

I put my hands on either side of the craft and pushed down as hard as I could. No luck. Because I was not familiar with exiting inverted, pinpricked hyphens in critical situations I could not get my legs into a position with which I could use them as leverage. Time was passing very slowly. My eyes were open and I could see the green water frothing about me.

It was pretty, but I was getting a bit tired of the view. I squirmed and squirmed to no avail. At long last, I stuck both hands above the surface and waved in all directions. To most kayakers, this is a distress signal, but I want to make it clear that I was not distressed. Since I was submerged, I knew my clever "last words" would never be heard and so I figured I might as well wave. I thought it would be nice for folks to have something to remember me by, and a snazzy "last wave" seemed sort of classy.

By this time, I was just plain perplexed. I simply could not figure out why I couldn't get out of the kayak. I was more angry than worried. Oh sure, I was about to drown, but it was the way I was about to drown that was so annoying. Drowning while executing a daring rescue, or trying to stop a flood, or even while trying to haul in a big fish, now those are noble ways to drown. But I was about to drown for a stupid reason and though I had done lots of things for stupid reasons in my life, I didn't want my death to be one of them.

A paddle tip suddenly brushed past my head and I felt something bump my kayak. Someone had come to keep me company. I was grateful for the companionship, but I was a little put out by the way whoever it was kept jabbing the tip of his paddle in my face. I was doing everything I could not to drown and this dolt was trying to knock me out with his paddle. Maybe it was the kayakers way of doing things, like shooting a horse with a broken leg. At long last, I could stand his rude intrusion no longer and so I reached up out of the water and laid hold to the front end of his kayak. With all my might, I pulled down, hoping to submerge his craft and teach him a lesson. The result was disappointing. As I pulled down on his craft my legs came free of my kayak, and I slipped out of the hole. His kayak hardly went under at all.

I took a breath and, though others claim I was gasping and sputtering, I said, "Well, if that's all there is to kayaking, I'll stick to canoeing." And then I dog-paddled and walked to shore.

The Art of
No-Hope Fishing

As far as I am concerned, the Fish, as an entity, has not been properly villainized in lore and legend. The Wolf, the Snake, and the Weasel have assumed places atop the list of cunning rouges and despotic tricksters in the animal world, but the Fish has, as of yet, escaped depiction as a dasher of human hope and joy.

Just as many animals, like wolves, snakes, and weasels, can sense fear, so fish can sense hope. Fish live to dash and destroy your hopes. They are slippery, crafty beasts who are waiting for you to want to catch them, to pin your very happiness on landing one of their kind. But all a fish wants is for you to be miserable and sad, your hopes and dreams lying around your feet like dried worms and broken driftwood. The trick, then, lies in hoping *not* to catch fish. Just as intelligence agents must deal in disinformation, so a true fisherperson must practice dis-hope.

My Uncle Rubin was one of the best fishermen I have ever known and it was all due to his sour hopelessness. Uncle Rubin practiced dis-hope from dawn to dawn. Like many great fisherman, Uncle Rubin was also a great theologian and was thus ready to defend his attitude of dis-hope with biblical references at any given moment. In fact, he was happiest when he could find no hope at all in scripture. He would shake his sagging head and say woefully, "So you don't believe that you have to have no hope to be a good a fisherman? Well, just go to the Good Book. Who were the Disciples? They were fishermen. And who were their forefathers? The very authors of the book of Lamentations. Those guys knew how to be distraught, and thus they caught fish."

"You take the story of the Great Catch in John 21, for example. Those guys had been in the boat fishing all night and had not caught a single thing. Then Jesus came to the edge of the water and said, 'Throw your net on the other side.' And they caught 152 fish! They were so good at being hopeless that it took divine intervention to net the fish. Now that is hopelessness. Fishermen need to get back to their roots of despair and depression." Then Uncle Rubin would frown and add, "Fish will always react counter to what you are hoping. You must learn to hope for just the opposite of what you want whenever you dare to cast your hook into the waters."

I have taken this attitude to heart and studied it in great detail along the banks of many rivers and on the shores of many lakes. Fish can read your hopes like the guy at the carnival who guesses your weight. They pick up your emotional vibrations as they drift underwater, transmitted along your ten-pound test like messages over a telegraph. Fish know exactly what you want and will almost always act in direct contradiction to your wishes. To illustrate this fact Uncle Rubin would glumly announce, "I'll bet you dollars to doughnuts that Jonah's last thought in the water was, 'I sure I hope I don't get swallowed up by a big fish.' And then BOOM! Right down the throat."

Furthermore, fish can morph into completely different incarnations in the blink of an eye. Many times I have sat listlessly by a dwindling fire on a riverbank, with a chunk of rotten liver lying beneath the surface only one cast away from me, when suddenly the grandfather of all catfish has picked up the bait and shot downstream at full speed. In my younger days, when I still openly hoped to land a record-breaking fish, I would jump to my feet, pole in hand, and steadfastly hope that I was bringing in a monster catfish. That hope would burn down the fishing line, right into that fish's mouth, and then he would smile. Having deduced that I wanted to catch a huge fish, and knowing that he was indeed a trophy catch, he would morph into a log or a tire. If he was feeling particularly mischievous, he would turn himself into a giant, ugly snapping turtle and rise out of the water like Death on a U-boat. Not only would this destroy my hopes, but it would generally leave me panicked and terrorized. I therefore set about to bury all trace of hope for fish deep within my breast.

Of course, I want to catch fish, you and I know that. What sane person doesn't want to catch fish? But what we must do is convince the fish that we do not want anything to do with them and are merely fishing out of need, as though it were a chore, like cleaning the toilet or eating vegetables. Make the fish believe that you would rather do anything but catch a fish and they will flock to you. Uncle Rubin would say, "Now boy, when you tie that hook onto your line, use a stout piece of loathing as a leader. And when you hook on that worm, slather it in lament as though you were buttering your morning toast."

Another benefit to this attitude of earnestly pretending to hate the act of fishing is that if you are good enough at faking dis-hope and despair, you might even convince your spouse that you hate the sport. Then he or she will allow you to fish with a willingness equal to his or her willingness to allow you to clean the toilet. Uncle Rubin had mastered the art of dis-hope to the point that he would say to his wife, my dear Aunt Gullible, with a deep sigh, "No, no honey. You stay home and weed the garden, clean the outhouse, wash the truck, and mow the lawn. I'll do the fishing."Then he would lift his rod like a soldier hefting his rifle to fight an unwinnable battle in a lost war. And she would hug him and say, "I'm sorry, honey, that you are the one who always has to go fishing. I love you for your selfless acts of kindness to your family."

Uncle Rubin was strict about his dis-hope rules. He would not fish with anyone who emitted positive vibes. Above the door at his fishing cabin there hung a sign that read,"Abandon All Hope of Catching Fish,Ye Who Enter Here."Utter any misplaced comment around the card table like, "Sure hope we catch some tomorrow," and Uncle Rubin would send you packing with a stern admonition that if you wanted to openly enjoy yourself, you could go to someone else's fishing camp.

The fishing cabin itself, however, was a wonderful testament to a life spent fishing well. On the wall, the wall that Uncle Rubin called his Wall of Shame when in earshot of any fish, even innocent goldfish and guppies swimming dumbly about in bowls, hung the trophies of his fishing philosophy. There were two-foot bass, trout the size of county fair First Place zucchini, a carp that you could have hollowed out to make a decent canoe, and then, on the floor and used by Uncle Rubin as a coffee table, lay a catfish three inches longer than his couch."Boys,"he would say, stretching his arms wide,"I never wanted to catch any of them. In fact, the day I caught that giant catfish I was hoping to get snagged on a log, lose my hook, and break my rod. Ruined my day when he broke the surface and pretty much jumped into my boat, laughing and croaking all the while. I would have thrown him back, except that I needed a coffee table and he looked to be about the right size."

When dawn broke, we would gather in the kitchen and Uncle Rubin would whip us up a mess of luke-warm coffee and half-a-dozen eggs. On non-fishing days, we had hot coffee and a dozen eggs for breakfast, but Uncle Rubin cut the ration in half on fishing days so that we might symbolically fast, and remember our sorrow. As we filed out the door, our heads hung low, he would give us each a piece of burlap, and a cigar. These were to sit on and to smoke, respectively, but they also served to remind us of sackcloth shirts, and ashes. And then he would whisper, so far under his breath that it came out as soft as the belly of a bunny, "Good luck, and good fishing. I hope you get a big one."

Jonah, The Last Two Chapters

Jonah, having been spit out by the fish, and having then taken care of his needs, heard the word of the Lord a second time. The Lord said, "OK, now get up and this time go to Halfdollar, that great city, and proclaim the message I will tell you." So, Jonah arose, and went to Halfdollar.

Halfdollar is a great city, but not a particularly large city. I know that it says in the Bible that the town was three days journey in breadth, but that is a mistranslation. What it really should say is that Halfdollar, because of recent problems at the sewer plant, smells like three-day-old breath.

Jonah went to the hardware store, rented a big white tent and a bunch of chairs, set them up in the park, and hung out a sign reading:

Revival!
7:30 PM!
Tonight!

That night, the whole town came out and gathered in the tent. Even the Mayor, who was not a particularly religious man, was there. It was, after all, an election year, and the Mayor was in need of votes. Everyone knew that the an official from the State Sanitation Board had inspected the sewer plant two days previously, and warned the Mayor that the plant was likely going to burst and flood the city in no more then six weeks, unless repairs were made immediately. The townsfolk held the Mayor responsible for the sewer plant problems. So, when Jonah took the stage and proclaimed, "Forty days and Halfdollar will be overrun!" the folks quickly did the math and figured out that Jonah was a prophet indeed, and that God was going to cause the sewer plant to burst in six weeks, overrunning them all in filth and waste if they did not change their ways.

They believed Jonah and they got down to business.

The Mayor, a practical man, realized that the best way to both please God and relieve the pressure on the sewer system was to call for all the townsfolk to go on a forty day fast. He published a column in the paper the next day proclaiming that no person, nor animal, should eat anything, or drink anything. As an added measure, he suggested that everyone should wear sackcloth and pray mightily to God. He also decreed that all sin should be kept to a minimum, and violence be halted for the time being. To that end, he recommended that folks unplug their televisions so that no one would be watching pro-wrestling or MTV. The Mayor finished his column by stating that he believed if the folks did all this, God might just repent, and let them live. And, the Mayor reminded the town, if God let them live they should all remember to vote for him come election day.

God, seeing how the people of Halfdollar repented, relented and did not cause their sewer plant to crumble.

Everybody was happy, except Jonah. Jonah, who had now been gone from home for sometime, and who had been thrown from a moving train, and swallowed by a river carp, was upset with God. Jonah said to God, "Look here, God. When you first told me that you wanted me to come here and preach to these folks, I knew you were going to save them anyway. That's why I tried to go to Grafton, instead. Now I've been gone from home for days and days, my lawn is probably out of control, my dog has probably run away, the stuff in my 'fridge is likely all gone moldy, I missed the opening day of baseball season, I'm sure my girlfriend has found someone new, and I haven't even started my taxes yet . . . I tell you God, just kill me now. It'd be better if I was dead."

The Lord said to Jonah, "Look here, moron, don't be mad at me. It's not healthy to use that tone of voice with me."

Jonah shuffled out of the city and built a booth to sit in so that he could watch what became of Halfdollar. While Jonah was sitting in his booth, the Lord appointed a kudzu plant to grow up around Jonah so that it might shade him, and keep him from burning in the sun. Jonah, though still miffed at God, was very happy about the plant. The next morning, however, Jonah awoke to the sound of a truck coming down the road. On the back of the truck there was a huge tank and nozzle that was spraying some sort of mist on the roadside plants. The spray fell all over Jonah's kudzu shade plant. Jonah noticed the words painted on the side of the truck read *Louden's Original Roadside Defoliant, Guaranteed, Outstanding, Dependable.* The acronym clearly spelling out *LORD GOD.* When the spray hit, Jonah's kudzu withered and died. And then God made the wind blow, and the sun beat down, and Jonah grew more and more agitated as he sweated in the sun. At last he said, "God, just let me die."

And God replied, "For the love of Pete! What is wrong now!"

And Jonah whimpered, "You took my kudzu shade plant."

And God said, "Look here, moron. You get yourself all bent out of shape for a plant that you neither created nor tended. It came into being overnight and died overnight. If you can get upset over that plant, why can't I get worked up about a city full of folks that I love, even if they don't know their right hand from their left? Besides that, there's a bunch of decent cattle in this town, and the high school has a heck of a football team. Now, quit whining and go home."

Jonah asked indignantly, "Go home? Just like that? You're not going to provide me a way home?"

And the Lord said, "I know a fish who is going your way."

Jonah smiled and said, "No thanks. I'll walk."

Dimes

On New Years Day, when I was eleven, I made a resolution. I decided what I wanted to be when I grew up. I wanted to be rich. And to be rich, I knew, you had to have one million dollars. So, I knew exactly what I had to do. I had to find, and save, one million dollar bills. How hard, I thought, could that be? It was my 1981 New Years resolution.

I started doing more chores around the house, I raked leaves for neighbors, I washed cars, I pulled weeds, I shoveled snow, and by the end of the first week I had collected and saved eight one dollar bills. At that rate I calculated it was going to take something like 125,000 weeks to become rich. Just for point of reference, that is 2403.84 years. Even if I factored in the odd $10 for a birthday here and there, it was obvious that I was not going to be able to collect enough one dollar bills to be rich by the time I was grown up. Clearly, I needed a new plan.

I decided that I would still go on earning and collecting one dollar bills while I was searching for a new idea, and so I went door-to-door asking folks if they would pay me a dollar for this or that. I got a great many dollars this way, and what I began to notice was that if I did a really fine job, people would invariably give me a little extra something for my troubles. That little extra something was usually a dime or two.

I would go home at night and put my dollar bills carefully in a shoebox, and then throw the dimes on my desk. One night, after I had counted my dollars—I had fourteen—I decided to count my dimes. I had sixteen. It occurred to me that people pretty much just gave dimes away. Dollars they hung on to, you had to work hard, for at least an hour, to get a dollar, but people just gave you dimes. I did some math. I needed only 10,000,000 dimes to be a millionaire. Now, by this time I was working about eight hours a week doing various tasks for people, and thus earning about eight dollars a week. What I realized was that if I did smaller jobs, and only charged a dime per job, I could probably squeeze as many as sixteen jobs into a week. That was sixteen dimes. I could, I realized, earn twice as many dimes in a week as I could dollars! I was off and running.

I decided it would be wise to turn my dollars into dimes, to turn my paper money into hard cash. I didn't, however, know exactly how to accomplish this. I had once heard my mother speak of a mythical place called *The Dime Store*. I wondered what sort of dimes they sold at *The Dime Store*, and how many you could buy for a dollar. It worried me that if there was such a place, it might mean that other folks had already struck on my get rich scheme. But I reckoned there were probably enough dimes to go around. The next day I searched the town high and low for *The Dime Store*, but it was nowhere to be found. It was, I figured, the Valhalla of dime men like myself. So, I put my dreams of a dime store to rest and took my fourteen one dollar bills to the bank where I cashed them in for dimes. The dimes, I found, cost about $1.20 a dozen. I now had 140 dimes from the bank, plus the sixteen I had at home, for a total of 156 dimes. That was more than ten times as many dimes as I had had dollar bills. I was rolling in the dough!

Neighbors practically lined up to have me wash their cars, sweep their basements, haul their garbage to the curb, walk their dogs . . . whatever. And all at a dime a shot. I would, if pressed, accept tips, but only dimes, never nickels or quarters. By the end of my first few months in my quest to be a millionaire I had gathered just over one thousand dimes. At most, I figured I could have only collected 150 dollar bills in that same amount of time. I was way ahead of the game.

I began collecting old bottles from streambeds and roadsides, all of which were worth a dime apiece. I'd stick my finger in every pay phone return coin slot and, from time to time would turn up a dime. One summer day my mom gave me two dollars. I went right to the store, bought some lemonade and paper cups, and set up a stand. I sold the lemonade for ten cents a cup and I turned those two dollars into 17 dimes.

Word got around town that I was collecting dimes, and kindly people would just hand them to me on the street.

Pretty soon my shoebox was overflowing with dimes. I could barely lift the box. I started filling coffee cans, mason jars, paper cups, anything that could hold a dime. I stashed them under my bed, in the closet, and in the drawers of my desk. I went into the attic and found an old, dry-rotted canvas duffle bag. I stood it in the corner of my closet and poured all my dime containers in that bag. For Christmas, all I asked for was dimes. No toys, no dollars, just dimes. My grandmother gave me 100 dimes, all in neat little paper rolls. My parents honored my wishes and gave me 500 dimes in a moneybag from the bank. Old St. Nick brought me another 500 dimes.

When I lost a tooth, I left a note for the Tooth Fairy.

It said, "Please, no quarters. Just dimes." It worked. Instead of the quarter I normally got for a tooth, I got two dimes. I am here to tell you that saints, folks, and fairies would much rather give you two or three dimes than a dollar, any day of the week. But, it's not nice to laugh. You know what they say, there's a sucker born every minute. It was hard for me to not become jaded in my wealth or to start taking advantage of people.

The day after Christmas, I started counting the dimes I had collected in the duffle bag. It took me a week. There was a sea of dimes stacked all across my bedroom floor. By the end of my first year in my quest to save 10,000,000 dimes, I had collected just shy of 10,000 dimes. When the sun shone through my window, the dimes which were spread across my floor sparkled and glittered like a great sequined dress. Any disco owner, this was the 80s after all, would have killed for my floor, but I wouldn't have traded my 10,000 dimes for $5,000.

I needed, I realized, to get the dimes out of my bedroom and into hiding. I spent a precious few of the dimes at the surplus store and bought four more canvas duffle bags. I put the duffels in the attic, and then slowly carried coffee can after coffee can of dimes up the attic stairs until I had five massive bags of dimes leaning beside the attic's trap door. I folded the stairs up, and went back to my room.

On I went, saving dimes, well into the summer.

And then, like in all great fiscal adventures, troubles arose. The first sign of trouble was what the papers called, "The Great Dime Shortage of 1982." I don't know how many dimes are supposed to be in circulation in any given town, but Halfdollar began to run out of dimes. Well, that's not exactly right. There were plenty of dimes in Halfdollar, it's just that they were all in my attic. People didn't want two nickels, or ten pennies for change. Customers started complaining to merchants about the dime shortage, and the merchants complained to the bank. The bank, I guess, complained to the U.S. mint, and they, apparently, called the Secret Service.

The next bump in my road to monetary bliss came when two agents from the Secret Service showed up in town one day and started working out the great dime caper. They questioned folks up and down the streets about where all the dimes had gone, and pretty soon, suspicion fell on me. Early one morning there was a knock on the door. I opened the door and found two well-dressed men showing me their badges.

"Son," they asked, "why are you hoarding dimes?"

"Dimes?" I asked, trying to look confused.

They stepped into the house.

The final trouble in my dime collection scheme started slowly. The agents were just inside the doorway of our house, at the base of the stairs, when my mother came into the hall. The agents were in the process of explaining to her what they were there for when something went "BUMP!" in the attic. The attic had one of those pull-down staircases that disappeared into the ceiling when you pushed it back up into place. Those pull-down stairs were located in the ceiling of the landing at the top of the stairs going from the first floor of our house to the second floor. The "BUMP!" we had all heard seemed to have come from that general direction.

"What was that?" the agents asked as they started up the stairs.

"That?" I asked. "Oh," I said, "that was just one of my dime bags."

The agent looked at me, puzzled. "Dime bags?"

"Yep," I confessed, "I have five of them."

"You have five dime bags?"

I nodded.

He looked at my mother and frowned. He asked me, "Is it grass? weed? coke? snow? angel dust? LSD?"

I nodded. I said, "Well, I cut grass, pulled weeds, hauled Coke bottles, and shoveled snow for them. I'm not sure about angel dust, but the Tooth Fairy helped me out some. And I don't know about LSD, I think its FDR."

"Partner," the first agent said to the second, "You'd better call the DEA."

And then, like water dripping through the ceiling, a dime fell through the attic's trapdoor, bounced on the landing, and then rolled down the stairs. We all stared at it. And then another dime dropped, and then another. The time between the dropping dimes grew shorter and shorter. Suddenly, a stream of dimes poured out of the attic and bounced down the stairs, and then, just as suddenly, the trapdoor sprang open, the fold-away stairs shot out, and a wave of dimes rolled down toward us. The agents were backing down the stairs when they were swept up in a rolling, bouncing, glittering avalanche of dimes. The wave pulled my mother and me with it. Twenty thousand dimes carried the G-men, my mother, and myself out the door. The dimes carried us halfway across the yard before they stopped. The four of us lay still. We were all exhausted from trying to keep afloat in the money. We were spent.

It is not illegal to collect dimes. It is not even illegal to hoard dimes, but Fate and Fortune can be cruel when you are twelve years old. I was only 9,980,000 dimes shy of my goal when the bottom fell out. I sat in the yard, under the glare of the two agents, my mother, and 20,000 images Franklin D. Roosevelt.

It took me the rest of that day, and most of the next, to shovel all of those dimes into the back of Dad's pickup truck. It took the bank nearly a week to count and roll all of those dimes. The bank manager asked me how I wanted the dimes converted. When I said, "Nickels, please," he nearly fainted. In the end, they gave me twenty-one hundred dollar bills. One hundred dollar bills are almost useless to a twelve-year old. My folks wouldn't let me do anything with them but put them in an interest-bearing account. "For your college education," they said.

When it was all said and done, I never got rich. I never got anything out of those dimes at all, except a college diploma. But what good is a diploma when you don't have a dime to your name?

Animal Escort

Recently, I went spelunking in a cave not far from my house. The cave is called Bowden Cave and is located just outside of Elkins, West Virginia. As I pulled into the parking lot at the cave, I was listening to a news bulletin on the radio. It made me giggle. Two bears had escaped from a circus in the area and were on the loose. These bears, the reporter said, were skilled at juggling beach balls while balanced on medicine balls. I laughed out loud as I parked my car in the parking lot just before dusk, turned off the lights, locked the doors and got out of my little hatchback Escort. I walked around to the back, opened the hatch, and got my gear, including a battery-operated headlamp, which I promptly fastened to my head. I then shut the hatch, double-checked that the car was locked, and headed into the cave.

Hours later, sometime just before eleven, I emerged from the cave wet, tired and hungry. I came up the path toward my car, headlamp still burning brightly, and, when I saw my car, I stopped dead in my tracks. This particular Escort is not what you would call a luxury vehicle. It is a 1995, manual transmission, four-door, hatchback, with 177,315 odd miles on it (and 32,412 even miles), and a dent in the backside. About the only cool feature of the car is that the backseat folds down at the press of a button, so that you can get into the hatch area without getting out of the car. The hatch area is covered by a hard plastic shelf so that passers-by cannot see what is stored in the back of the car. Fancy, huh? And yet, someone had decided to loot my car while I was in the cave. The hatch was open, the driver's side front door was open, and the passenger side back door was open. In anger, I slammed the hatch shut and walked around to the driver's seat, fishing my keys out of my pocket. When I tried the ignition, it was just as I had expected. With the doors open, the dome light had been on, and thus the battery had died.

Discouraged, I began to inspect the interior of the car to see what, if anything, was missing. There wasn't much to steal. I had had a box of instant porridge and loaf of bread on the front seat, a cooler with some sandwiches in the backseat, and not much else. I turned my head toward the passenger seat, headlamp beaming, and found that the box of porridge was torn open, and the loaf of bread had been opened and ravaged by a skunk. How did I know that a skunk had done it? Well, just like in the story of Goldilocks, something had found my porridge too cold, and found my bread to be just right. And she was still there. Sound asleep.

Startled at the sight of a skunk curled up on the passenger seat of my looted car, I did what any good woodsman would do. I screamed and jumped into the backseat. The scream woke the skunk. The jump, well, the landing from the jump, woke the bear. You see, a black bear had climbed in the open back door, opened my cooler, eaten my sandwiches, and fallen asleep across the backseat. When I landed on his back, still screaming from the sight of the skunk, the bear instantly stood. When he stood, with me laying upside down on his back, he crushed my face into the top of the car. So, there I was, in the backseat of my looted car, squished between the felt of the ceiling and the pelt of bear while a skunk looked over the front seat, tail raised.

The bear saw the skunk. The skunk saw the bear. The bear then began trying to get out of the car. The trouble was, he was wedged in pretty good between me and the seat, and he was facing the left rear door, which was closed. He had, please remember, come in the right rear door. Noticing that I had left the front, driver's side door open, the bear began wiggling himself over the front seat. As he pressed his way through the narrow space, he managed to peel me off his back. I fell, relieved, onto the backseat. The skunk, however, seeing the bear coming into the front seat, naturally jumped into the backseat with me. Thinking quickly, I pressed the lever that released the backseat, folded it down, rolled into the enclosed hatch area, and pulled the seat back up before the skunk could follow me. I took a deep breath and tried to relax.

I felt the springs of the car bounce up as the heavy bear stepped out of the car. Now it was just me and the skunk.

As I had climbed into the hatch area, I knocked my headlamp on something and it went out. Needless to say, it was cramped and dark in the hatchback area of my little '95 Escort. Reaching around blindly, looking for some sort of weapon, my hand fell on something warm, round and rough. I knew I had a thick coil of rope in the back somewhere and I figured it would make as good a weapon as anything. I grabbed hold of the rope and tried to position myself in such a way as to be able to bust through the backseat, swat the skunk, and roll free before the impending blast. When I rolled, I heard a rattle.

Now, I have a young child. He tends to leave toys laying about and I was not unused to stepping on, kicking, rolling over onto, and otherwise causing the toys to accidentally whistle, ring, and rattle, without warning. Thus, I did not give the rattle a second thought.

Holding the rope, I braced myself and got ready to kick through the seat. Just then, the springs of the car sunk once, and then twice, as if not one, but two large creatures had crawled into the car. Perplexed, I decided to go about my plan and deal with any new developments after I had taken care of the skunk. I tightened my grasp on the rope, rolled on the rattle again, and kicked with all my might. The seat flew forward, I swung the coiled rope around fast, bumped the headlamp again, which caused it to re-light, and then I screamed.

When I kicked out of the hatch, the skunk had flown into the front of the car and landed on the dashboard. He was now standing, tail poised and ready for attack. Staring over the headrests of the front seat were the huge heads of two bears. They had apparently smelled the food and crowded in the front door to see what was to be had. The rattle sounded again. But I hadn't moved. The rope in my hand, however, had. I looked up to see that I was holding a rattlesnake by the neck, and he was looking alternately between me, the bears, and the skunk; tongue flicking, fangs dripping. The rattlesnake had a large lump in his neck, as though he had recently eaten. I did what any man would have done. I threw the snake into the front seat, rolled back into the hatch, and pulled the backseat closed. I was quite willing to let the snake, the skunk, and the bears work out their differences alone.

There were grunts, hisses, growls, and yelps from the front seat. The car shook, rocked, bounced, and then started to roll. I knew what had happened, had even expected it. One of the bears, during the struggle, had released the parking brake, and now we were rolling downhill. Me in the trunk, and the two bears, the snake, and the skunk up front.

There were a number of thumps on the exterior of the car as we started to roll. Best as I could figure, we'd hit some trees with the open doors, knocking the doors shut. Now the five of us were sealed in good. We began gaining speed. Faster and faster we rolled downhill. I knew, even if the animals didn't, that there was a sharp curve at the bottom of the hill, and if one of them didn't start steering, we were in for quite a crash. If we didn't make the curve, we were going to be headed right toward the river. I had a pal, who everybody called Shake, that lived on the river right below that curve. He had just built a nice dock out into the river and, if we didn't make the turn, we were going to crash through the guardrail, past Shake's house, across his dock and into the water. If that happened, I was sure I would drown.

Sure enough, we crashed through the wooden guardrail and started bumping across Shake's lawn. Come what might, I had to get out of the trunk before we went into the water. I quietly let the backseat down and peered out. The skunk was still on the dashboard, staring straight ahead, the snake, with the lump in his throat, was coiled around the rearview mirror, and the bears were wide-eyed and tense. It was just then that I noticed all the beach balls in the car. Obviously, these were the juggling bears that had escaped from the circus. As I was taking all of this in, there was a tremendous crash, thump, and a shattering of glass. We had run straight into my pal Shake's pigpen, and slammed into one of his boars. The boar rolled up the hood and through the windshield, crushing the skunk. The skunk, after all that time, finally sprayed her musk. The car filled with the pungent smell as it clouded around us. It was so bad that the snake threw up. The little lump in the snake's throat popped out of his mouth in the form of a swallowed, soiled, shaken, but still living shrew.

The shrew, glad to have escaped, dove down under the steering wheel. The bear in the driver's seat, startled by the boar coming through the window, the skunk spraying, the snake upchucking, and the shrew jumping between his legs, starting flailing his feet just as we rolled out onto Shake's dock. In a miraculous turn of events, the bear hit the brakes and we screeched to a stop just at the edge of the dock.

Shake, having heard all the racket and seen his boar run over, had called the cops. The cops showed up just as the escaped circus bears, who seemed unfazed by all the commotion, retrieved their beach balls, perched themselves on their medicine balls, and started juggling.

The officers who arrived just shook their heads as I explained the whole story. I was in a lot of trouble, they said. First of all, I was informed that I was responsible for the death of the skunk that had, of course, been boared to death. When the cops saw the two escaped bears, they naturally assumed that I had kidnapped, or bear-napped, the bears. So I got a hefty ticket for bear-napping, which, by the by, is not the same thing as hibernation. And at last, the cops said I was a very, very lucky man. They explained that if it hadn't been for the timing of the shrew, I would have certainly gone off Shake's pier.

Of Chicken Wieners and Fathers-in-Law

By nature, fathers-in-law are decent and loyal, but they have been bred to protect their daughters as their most valuable possessions. This is all good, provided you are a son-in-law with your papers, shots, and morals in proper working order. In the beginning, it is perhaps best to approach your father-in-law with the same respect and openness you would grant to a guard dog or sentinel lion. Advance slowly, don't make any sudden movements, keep your hands where he can see them, and don't try sneaking into or out of any windows. Most important, allow the relationship to grow over time. Don't expect him to forget his noble vigil overnight. Oh, and get a haircut.

I have ten years' experience with a father-in-law. He is the only one I have ever had and he is a fine guy. We have always been polite and amiable toward one another, but lately we have grown still closer. Maybe it is because I have aided him in his plight to rid his yard of armadillos, or perhaps it because I am partially responsible for giving him his first grandson. Or maybe it has something to do with the fact that he knows that in times of crisis, when actions speak louder than words (actually, I have noticed that some words always speak louder than actions), when success and failure hang in the balance by the thinnest of lines, I can be depended on to do the right thing. Obviously, I am referring to fishing.

Recently, my father-in-law, who I call C.G., has done most of his fishing at Simmons, which is a catfish farm. You don't have to worry about mosquitoes and the fish come already filleted and frozen, but it lacks some of the adventure of big fish hunting. So, when I went down there this past month, C.G. was itching to catch some real, still thawed, catfish from the river itself.

Directly behind my in-laws' house flows the Big Sunflower River. The Big Sunflower, however, is a tricky river to fish. You will not, barring massive geological and meteorological shifts of glacial and volcanic proportions, ever find the Big Sunflower on any list of the most pristine rivers in the world, unless that list is called "The Most Pristine Rivers in Mississippi called The Big Sunflower." Casting into the river is akin to casting into a willow tree, so you have to be creative in your tactics.

I'm not sure where the term *trotline* originated, but I strongly suspect that its derivation comes from an acronym used to help remember an early Scot-Irish haiku, penned when those settlers first cast a line into the Big Sunflower. I believe the haiku goes:

Tangled my new line.

Rats, hung on a sunken limb.

Oh @#*$! Tarnation!

The trotline is a clever device for fishing a river like the Big Sunflower because from the beginning, in a sense, your line is already snagged at both ends, so the river will pretty much leave you alone. What's more, you don't have to spend all day fighting snags and snarls.

As I said, C.G. had a hankering to land a fish and so he was ready to go fishing as soon as my wife and I tumbled out of the car. C.G. had what he called a craw-fish rake in the back of his truck, and he and I headed out to see if we could nab some bait.

"It's a little late in the season for crawfish," C.G. was saying as we drove through the cotton fields and toward the forest, "but they're the best bait I know for catfish. Mr. Jim lent us this rake and his big fishing net."

"Who's Mr. Jim?" I asked.

"He's an older fella, you probably met him at church, but he used to do a bunch of fishing when he was younger. Loved catfish. Ate fried catfish every day, until he had his heart attack. Then his cardiologist told him he could only eat it twice a month. That nearly killed him. He owns that johnboat down at the house. He did most of his fishing right behind our house."

"He used a trotline?" I asked.

"Yep. Said crawfish were the best bait, but he said if we couldn't get any crawfish to use chicken wieners instead."

My father-in-law is fond of tricking people, especially Yankees like myself. He was driving home from a National Guard exercise one time, a Yankee in the passenger seat of his truck. "That fella," explained C.G., "fell asleep and was snoring up a storm. His snoring was drowning out the Braves game on the radio. So, I noticed up ahead of us, on the highway, that there was one of those tow trucks that tow the cabs of eighteen wheelers, only they tow them backwards so that it looks like they are coming right at you. I drove right up under the grill of that towed cab, right between the headlights, and then I screamed at the top of my lungs! That ol' boy woke up, saw that truck coming right at us, jumped clean into the backseat, and never fell asleep in a truck I was driving again."

That story in mind, I approached the notion of chicken wieners cautiously. "C.G.," I said, "unless I am woefully mistaken, chickens don't have wieners."

C.G. looked at me like I was crazy. He squinted, and then it dawned on him. "No, no," he chuckled, "not chicken's wieners. I mean hot dogs made out of chicken." We laughed. He would have tricked me, if he'd been thinking about it.

"How do we catch the crawfish?" I asked.

"It's pretty easy. All you do is stick that rake out in the water and drag it back to you along the surface of the ditch."The crawfish rake consisted of a ten-foot aluminum handle welded to a basket made of chicken wire. "If you get out here at the right time of the year, you can fill that basket up in one scoop. But, like I say, it's a little late in the season."

The area we were driving through was part of a large tract of public land maintained for outdoor recreation of most any sort. In the winter months the low ground was flooded, thus producing habitat for both birds and fowl hunters. C.G., who had retired from the Forest Service after forty odd years, was explaining how flooding the forest was beneficial to the trees and undergrowth. He also said that when they drained the forest in the spring a lot of water stayed behind, filling the ditches by the sides of the roads. Crawfish, at certain times of the year, flourish in these waters and, because they are trapped, are easy prey for animals and humans alike. We pulled to a stop by a sloppy pool trapped in the raised, convex corner of a crossroads.

"If they're anywhere," C.G. said, "there'll be some out there, but it's really too late in the season."

There were two small crawfish in the hole. And two more in another ditch.

"Looks like chicken wieners," C.G. said.

We rode back to the house and C.G. got the wieners out of the refrigerator. We cut them up into chunks and walked down to the river where we loaded up the little boat and pushed out into the muddy waters. C.G. paddled the boat a little ways upstream and we found a place to tie off the line. He made certain that the line was fairly well hidden. "Some folks will come along and check the line for you, if you don't hide it," he said. He paddled the boat as directly across the river as the current would allow as I baited hooks and dropped them into the flow. We attached a weight in the middle of the line and then tied it to the limb of a fallen, partially submerged, tree. After that, we paddled upstream a dozen yards and set out another line. We put our four crawdads in a row along the middle of the second trotline. Then we drifted back to the house. We spent the next four days checking and re-baiting our lines.

In this world there are many fathers and sons who could not spend hours in a small boat together, and I reckon there are many more sets of male in-laws who couldn't either. Some wouldn't even try. I guess I could moralize, and say that what really matters is that C.G. and I get along and that that is a reward all its own, but why would a man moralize when he could brag that he and his father-in-law caught a thirty-pound catfish on a chicken wiener?

Engine Blockhead

I am not a strong man. My biceps don't stretch the fabric of my sleeves, my chest is slightly concave, my legs are bowed and rubbery, and the closest my abdomen muscles have ever been to "washboard" was the time I belly flopped onto a steel grate. We were cooking burgers on the grate and while I was mostly unhurt, I did have a nice crisscross pattern on my stomach for sometime. From a distance, the marks looked like the shadows cast by firm belly muscles. But eventually the marks faded and I was left as weak as ever. Still and all, I am fit and healthy and thus go about doing manly things, despite my frail physique.

I hunt and fish with a group of buddies who are basically nice guys, except that they are all fitness nuts who work out and jog. They are all ex-Army men. They like to brag of their strength and tell long stories about how they had to lift, pull, drag, carry, or hurl fallen trees, bagged game, stuck trucks, charging beasts, or each other through various circumstances in which their brawn always proved to be the savior of all things right, good, and decent. When finished field dressing a deer, they always throw it over their shoulders and hike back to camp, often choosing the longest and most difficult trail in order to have more material to brag about. I compensate for this by being a terrible shot. In their eyes it is more honorable to be a poor marksman than to drag, rather than carry, a deer through the woods.

My buddies call me their"Little Weak-end Warrior." That stings. My end is not all that weak. I have proved that to them on more than one occasion after eating sauerkraut and sausage. They offer to tote my pillow for me so I won't hurt my back.

I sometimes feel inferior to them and thus I find myself testing my own strength, when no one else is around. In my backyard I sometimes pick up whole cinder blocks and chuck them as far as I can, being careful not to hit my feet.

One day, it came to be that I was at our local auto parts store. I had asked for an apparently rare piece of machinery because the clerk had left the desk for the backroom to look for the part and had been gone a good half hour. I casually strolled through the store while I waited, checking out every piece of merchandise until I was thoroughly bored.

I went and stood next to the counter, tapping my fingers. While I was standing there I noticed a big sign sitting atop a box. The sign read, "We Now Carry Engines." The box was a cube, three feet by three feet. It was a bright red box and on each side it had a drawing of an engine. Across the top of each side were the words, "Four Cylinder 1.6 Liter Engine." The box was sitting on a pallet of rough oak.

I looked around the store. The clerk was still in the back and there were no other customers. I examined the box from where I stood, to see if there was any indication of how much the engine weighed. I tilted my head to read the fine print, but there was no clue. I was wondering if I could lift an engine. I strolled over to the box and tapped the pallet with my foot. It didn't budge. I walked down the nearest aisle, trying to think of other things beside lifting that engine. It was a stupid idea. I could barely propel an Internet search engine. My thoughts kept drifting back to the idea though. Boy, would I be able to brag to my buddies if I could lift that engine. I turned down the next aisle and headed back toward the box.

As I drew closer, I scanned the store again for signs of other people; there was no one else in the place. I decided that my clerk must have gone to Detroit to get my part. I had the place to myself. I strutted up to the box, circled it, and then squatted. I knew enough to lift with my knees. I grasped the underside of the pallet with both hands, shoulder length apart, rolled my neck muscles, flexed my shoulders, looked around one more time, took a deep breath, held it, and then with a great exhalation, I lifted with all my might.

To my great surprise, the pallet came off the floor. The sign announcing "We Now Carry Engines" soared into the nearest aisle and skittered across the tile. I had put so much force into my lift that I could not counter my action before the pallet had lifted completely off the ground and the engine and the pallet were cart wheeling across the showroom floor. The pallet veered into a display of motor oil and dozens of black plastic bottles toppled to the floor and slid in all directions. The engine bounced and rolled. I couldn't believe my eyes. Not only had I lifted the engine, but I had sent it tumbling, pistons over spark plugs, across the store. The box skidded to a stop upside down, just in front of the battery display.

I looked around again, smiling broadly, now wishing that there had been someone in the store to see my superhuman feat. I checked to see if there were any surveillance cameras in the store. I thought maybe I could get a copy of the tape. I swaggered over to the engine and looked at my handy work. The box was dented on the corners. I hoped I hadn't broken the thing, I didn't need an engine. Especially a broken one. I left the engine where it was and started cleaning up a bit. I put the pallet back in place and tried to rebuild the wall of oil bottles I had displaced. That done, I sauntered back over to the engine. Knowing full well that I was more than strong enough to toss that little 1.6-liter engine around, I grabbed the box in both hands and lifted with a quick jerk. The box came off the ground like it was empty, and I fell backwards, the box landing square on my weak stomach. Nothing. I wasn't crushed to death. My braggadocio-filled muscles started sending confused messages to my brain. My brain simply opened the floodgates and all the vanity I had acquired in the past few minutes spilled out, and ignominy rushed in to fill the void. Enough humility poured forth from my soul to fill the empty box on my stomach, three times over.

I got up, set the "engine" back on the pallet and left the store without the part I had intended to buy. I knew I wouldn't be working on the car that day. I had sprained my ego and I needed to lie down.

Falsecium Abidebyme: Part I?

Falsecium abidebyme (the real name of the chemical has been changed to protect the stupid) and water
produce asettling gas (the name of the gas has been
changed to protect those same idiots as above).
Asettling gas is flammable, even explosive.

The first time Skeet and I ever bought falsecium was
at Sullivan's Flea Market. Sullivan's is the closest thing
we ever had to a mall in Halfdollar, West Virginia. It
has everything a mall has, right down to a food court,
if a crock-pot full of hot dogs floating in greasy water
can be considered a food court. We were fifteen years
old and ready for something new. Sullivan always
seemed to know when we had an itching for some new
diversion, and he always had the cure.

"Boys," Sullivan said, "have I got something for you."
He was holding a shiny tin can with dangerous black
lettering. I say the lettering was dangerous because it
was obviously either industrial or military. Simple
script, printed right on the can. No paper label, and no
hint of a marketer's influence. It ing that let the buyer
know that this was the sort of product bought by people
who knew exactly what they wanted. It was the very
same lettering and script used on cases of dynamite.
People who buy dynamite know what they want and

don't care about slick advertising. The boxes just say, in a plain font, "Dynamite. Handle with Care. Explosive. Not to be sold to minors." And so it was with the can of falsecium abidebyme Sullivan held in his hand.

"Boys," he said, "I shouldn't even be showin' y'all this."

Sullivan knew how to work us. Ever since we were just little kids Skeet and I would go to Sullivan's with pockets full of quarters and he would say things like, "Now fellas, this is very sharp," or, "Now son, don't let yer mommas know I showed you this." Our eyes wide, we would hand him our money. With Sullivan around, Skeet and I didn't need drugs.

"This here is falsecium abidebyme. It says right on the can 'Splosive. Lord knows why I'm even lettin' y'all know I got this 'cause I sure ain't gonna sell it to ya."

The can did indeed have the word "explosive" stenciled on it in neat black letters. And the word "warning," and the word "dangerous," and the word "flammable." My mouth went dry. Skeet's eyes bugged out. Between all those words, in the same dangerous lettering, was a chemical formula: $Fals2+CIuM2H2OH - FA- H+Fal(OH)2$. We had no idea what it meant, but it was a chemical formula, and that could only mean good things.

"This here falsecium abidebyme," Sullivan continued, "is what the coal miners used in their headlamps before they invented bat'ry powered lights and strung 'lectricty in the mines. They'd take a falsecium lamp, just like this one here," he paused and picked up an old brass lamp from beside him. "You ever seen one of these 'fore?"

"Yes sir. In school."

The falsecium lamp is a magnificent thing. It is a simple device used by cavers, and coal miners before that. A falsecium lamp has three main parts; the chemical canister, the water reservoir, and the reflector. To make it work, you simply put a handful of falsecium abidebyme in the bottom part and fill the top half with water. Gravity pulls the water slowly through a dripper. The water drops onto the falsecium, and the resulting chemical reaction produces asettling gas. The gas then drifts up a tiny pipe and is channeled to a gas outlet centered in the reflector. On the reflector is a simple flint and steel sparker, just like you would find on a Zippo lighter. You simply flick the sparker, the sparks ignite the gas, and voilà, you have a three-inch smokeless flame. The flame is reflected in the concave reflector and you can see in the dark.

"Good," Sullivan said. "Anyway, they take the lamp and unscrew it." He unscrewed the base. "Drop in some falsecium." Using a pocketknife, he pried the lid off the shiny can with the dangerous lettering and showed us the contents. The can was full of little, pea-sized chunks of gray, chalky falsecium abidebyme. It looked like gravel. Sullivan then dumped a few chunks of it into the lamp. "Then they screwed the bottom back on, like this. And then you pour a little water in the top." He did. "Wait a second." A slight hissing noise escaped from the lamp. Sullivan cupped his hand over the reflector for a moment, and then, with a quick motion, he pulled his hand away, striking the flint and steel sparker. A flame shot forth. Skeeter and I could not have been more impressed had Sullivan turned water into wine, or made 3,000 fish out of three. Sullivan had made fire from water and gravel. He laughed a little, smiling. He knew he had us. We knew he had us. And we were glad to be had.

"How much?" Skeet asked.

"Oh, it'll burn half an hour, whole hour if you add some more water."

"No," I asked, dazed, dry mouthed, palms sweating, "how much for the can of falsecium abidebyme?"

"No, sir. No way." Sullivan laid the lamp down, the tiny flame still jutting out. He lifted the lid of the falsecium can off the table, laid it over the opening of the can and tapped it shut with a hammer. "No way boys. I told you already, yer mommas would kill me if they even knew I showed it to you."

"She'll never know," Skeet said. "I won't tell her."

"And I won't tell mine." Skeet and I were staring at the flame. Our voices came out low, slow, and monotone, as though we were under a spell.

"They'd know al'right, sure they would. Soon as y'all come in the house all burned up, hands singed, clothes smolderin'. Oh they'd know."

I cleared my throat. "How much?"

"Well, boys. I tell you what. I paid five dollars for this can. I can make y'all a deal though. I can let it go to y'all for fourteen."

"Fourteen? How do you figure?" Skeet asked.

"Insurance. See, if y'all do blow each other up, or the town for that matter, why the FBI will trace that can right back to me. And then they'll sue me for damages. I gotta have that extra nine dollars for damages." He picked up the can and handed it to Skeet.

Skeet hefted it. Shook it, read all that dangerous lettering, and reached in his pocket. He had six tattered ones and four quarters. I had a ten.

"OK then. Seventeen it is." Sullivan grabbed the money.

"Wait. You said fourteen."

"That was b'fore tax. There's a three dollar federal 'splosives tax on that falsecium abidebyme."

Skeet and I were fifteen-years-old. We couldn't be snowed by Sullivan as easily as we might have when we were seven or eight. I took a deep breath, trying to regain my senses after being blinded by the miracle of fire. I rubbed a little spit into my eyes and tried them again. Sure enough, my insights were returning as rapidly as my outsights. We were dumb, but not stupid. We knew Sullivan had been bilking us for extra quarters and dimes all our lives, and now we were ready to get a little payback. "OK," I said. "That sounds fair. But," now it was our turn to bargain a little, "you have to give us two falsecium lamps."

"Do what?" Sullivan asked. "Them lamps is 'spensive. More than you can afford."

"Well," Skeet said, hefting the can, shaking it, "I reckon if we had them lamps we could go out and use this falsecium like we're supposed to. Without the lamps, well, you just got done implying we could blow stuff up if we wanted."

"In fact," I added, "I believe you explained to us exactly how to do it."

"I never did." Sullivan said.

"No. I guess not. But I'll tell my momma you did." I said.

"Yeah, after we blow up the sewer system or something, accidentally of course, why I'll just tell Sheriff Hasbro where we got the stuff to do it with." Skeet smiled, shook the can.

"Boys," Sullivan said, "You gettin' right tricky as you come up. I reckon you're a might smarter than I give ya credit for. How 'bout this? Them lamps cost me twenty-five dollars. Apiece. You done give me seventeen already. If y'all give me another twenty-five, I'll give you two lamps and throw in the falsecium for free. How's that sound?"

Skeet and I conferred. That was a lot of money, but one had to consider the possibilities.

"What about helmets? To put the lamps on?" Skeet asked.

"Got them, too."

I said, "Let's see 'em."

Sullivan got up from his chair and walked to the back of his shop. He came out with two battered hard hats, each having a device on the front into which the lamps slid. And, each having a price tag reading $1.25.

"Right," I said, "We'll take the whole lot of it for another twenty-five bucks."

"Not these helmets too, no sir." Sullivan said righteously." They cost twenty apiece."

"Mr. Sullivan," Skeet said, pointing to the price tags, "those tags say $1.25, and they say, in smaller letters, Sullivan's Flea Mkt."

"Damn," was the best he could do. "Al'right, ya give me seventeen dollars already, give me twenty-five more and we'll call it even."

I reached in my sock and pulled out a five. Skeet found a twenty in his shoe. We handed it over, grabbed the helmets and the lamps, and ran. It was best to just get out quick. If you looked at the transaction from a strictly financial standpoint, it was difficult to say who got the better end of the deal, us or Sullivan. Moneywise, both parties probably came up short, but, on the other hand, Skeet and I had two hard helmets, two falsecium lamps, and a can full of contents for which a lot, a whole lot, of dangerous lettering was required.

We went straight to Skeet's garage. The first thing we did was load up the lamps with falsecium and water, and light them. We practiced lighting them and then blowing them out, and then relighting them with our eyes closed. It seemed prudent to be skilled at that task if we were going to be cavers, spelunkers.

"OW!" Skeet said.

I opened my eyes. "What?"

"I burned myself."

"How?"

"Checking to see if the flame was burning. I stuck

my hand in front of the reflector. Burned me good."

"Why didn't you just look to see if the flame was burning?"

"Duh," he said, "we had our eyes shut to practice starting the lamps in the dark. How else was I going to check?"

"Skeet," I said mildly, "once we relight the lamps, down there in the dark of the cave, it won't be dark any longer. The whole point of the light is that we can see it."

"Shut up, will ya?" he asked.

After that, we took the lamps, attached them to our helmets, and climbed down into the crawlspace under Skeet's house. Sure enough, those little lights cast out a whole lot of light. The neat thing was that the light was focused in front of you. It wasn't like a lantern. Lanterns give off plenty of light, but lantern light leaks out all over the place, and never right where you want it. The falsecium lamps attached to our helmets put out light like a flashlight beam; there was even a circle of light on the wall ahead of us. And, with the lamp fastened on the helmet, your hands were free, so you could crawl about without a care in the world. We were under the house for a good hour. We came out when the lamps started to sputter.

We went back to the garage and removed the lamps from our helmets. We set the lamps on the worktable and stared at them. The little yellow flames were now only half an inch long, and they were struggling. Every now and then one or the other would shrink until it was just a pinprick of yellow, and then leap out again. And then, without fanfare or explosion, the two small flames vanished into the lamps.

"Let's play with falsecium," Skeet said.

We dumped a few chunks on the floor and poured a bit of water on the pile. The chunks fizzled and seemed to steam.

"That must be the gas coming off," Skeet said.

I lit a match and tossed it at the pile. A flame as big as my forearm leapt up, and then disappeared just as quickly. I did it again. The second flame was smaller, the third smaller still. Skeet poured more falsecium onto the floor, then water. This time he threw a match. Flash.

"Man," I said, "this is good stuff."

"Maybe," Skeet said thoughtfully, "we should go outside."

We played around with the falsecium, water, and matches until dinnertime, and then we grabbed the lamps from the worktable and went into Skeet's house. We took the lamps into the bathroom and opened them up. The water was gone from the tops, and, down below, the falsecium abidebyme had turned into a substance like wet sand. Knocking the bottom of the lamps against the toilet bowl, we were able to get most of the spent falsecium out of the lamps. It dropped into the commode with a splash. Using a nail file, we were able to scrape the remaining dregs into the john. We shut the toilet lid and left the bathroom. Halfway down the hall we passed Frank, Skeet's dad, heading toward the bathroom.

Frank smokes. Skeet and I were just topping the stairs when we heard a BOOM. And then a CRACK. And then a "YELP!" Right away I couldn't account for the boom and the crack, but the yelp had been Frank. No doubt about it.

"Uh-oh." I whispered to Skeet. We had stopped on the top of stairs when we heard the sounds.

"Sounds like maybe Dad blew up. That ain't good. The question is, was it our fault and how do we get out of it. We can't ignore it, it was too loud. Chances are, it was our fault. But we have to go see. Hopefully, Mom will get there before us and she might protect us."

"You never know," I said.

We stashed the lamps in Skeet's room and ran back to the bathroom. Frank was standing over the john scratching his head. The lid of the toilet was cracked in two, and half of it was laying on the floor. That would have been the CRACK.

Frank said, "Well, I'll be go to hell," very quietly, like he was doing long division in his head.

"What happened, Dad?"

"I don't know. I walked in here, took a drag on my cigarette," Frank pantomimed smoking, his thumb and forefinger squeezed tightly in front of his lips, "I took it out of my mouth, stepped to the toilet," Frank stepped to the toilet, "lifted the lid, just a little," he pretended to lift the lid, "tossed in the burning butt of my cigarette, and, well, BOOM!"

"You been eatin' beans, Mr. Barth?" I asked.

He smiled. He reached in his breast pocket and pulled out a pack of smokes.

"Dad," Skeet asked, "do you think that's a good idea? Could be a gas leak or something, right?"

"Well," Frank was thinking out loud, "toilets are designed to not let gas back in, same with sinks. Hmmm." He scratched his head, put his cigarette in his mouth, and got out his lighter. Frank was a little single-minded. He knew that somehow his lit cigarette had touched off a small explosion in the bathroom. He knew that somehow those two things were connected, but he was so focused on the principle at hand, his blowing up the toilet with a burning cigarette, that it never crossed his mind that lighting a second cigarette might touch off a similar explosion. He thumbed his lighter. I backed out of the bathroom, cringing. Nothing. He lit his smoke. Nothing. He took a healthy drag. Nothing. The tip of the cigarette glowed bright red. He said, "Good Lord! What am I doing!" He tore the cigarette from his mouth and threw it at the toilet, to extinguish it. Realizing his folly he then lunged for it. The cigarette hit the water with a quiet "plop . . . fzzzzz." Nothing happened. Frank said, "Well, I'll be go to hell," and scratched his head. He reached for his breast pocket and pulled out another cigarette.

I nudged Skeet and motioned him to come on. Frank might deliberate all day. The best thing to do was not be around. So far suspicion had not fallen in our direction and I aimed to keep it that way. If Skeet and I stayed in the bathroom long enough, one or the other of us would eventually say something that would clue Frank in to our guilt. We backed out of the bathroom, down the hall, and up the stairs.

When we were in his room Skeet said, "Well, what have we learned from all of this?"

I shrugged, "Don't throw falsecium abidebyme in the toilet and forget to flush?"

"Yes," Skeet nodded, "I hadn't considered it from that angle, but what I mean is, what important, useful thing have we learned?"

I shrugged.

He said, "We learned, first and foremost, that if you allow the asettling gas produced by the falsecium to collect in a confined space, a closed toilet for example, it will not just burn, but explode." We both started to chuckle, and then laugh. No wonder Sullivan had said our mothers would kill him if he sold the stuff to us.

It was dinnertime and I had to head home. Under our share-and-share-alike policy it was agreed that we should divide the remaining falsecium in half. I would take half home with me, and Skeet would keep half. We had instituted this policy less because of lack of trust and more due to the search and seizure policy of our folks. It was not unusual for our folks, in the name of county-wide tranquility, to search our respective bedrooms. Yes, it was unconstitutional and morally wrong, but it was also the 1980s and nobody cared yet about my rights. Especially the citizenship-at-large of Halfdollar, West Virginia. If my folks, or Skeet's folks, wanted to search a bedroom in the house they owned, well, the Circuit Judge, Sheriff, and Pastor themselves would be glad to oblige or assist in any way possible. So, Skeet and I divided and stashed everything in the hopes of preserving at least half of anything we shouldn't have. Skeet went down to the kitchen and came back with an empty canning jar.

"I washed it out," he said. "Who knows what would happen if you mixed falsecium with Mom's field peas." We dumped about half of the remaining falsecium in my canning jar and then taped the lid on with masking tape.

"Look," I said to Skeet, "I can't just strut through your mom's kitchen with this jar. She'll look in it."

Because it was just good sense to know everything humanly possible about what me and Skeet where up to, it was also common practice for our folks to search us before we left the house, especially if we were carrying things like canning jars full of gravel. One could carry a plethora of dangerous things in a canning jar— be they living, liquid, mineral, or dead. You could also, of course, put foodstuffs in canning jars, if you had no better use for the jar.

"So? She won't know what it is," he said, shrugging.

"Skeet, how many times have we said that?"

"Yeah, I know. And really, it's worse when she doesn't. I mean, if she opens a can and there is a dead squirrel in it, well, she knows what that is. She can handle that. But she'll take one look at that jar, see some innocent-looking gravel, and know something is really wrong."

"Right," I added.

"And, if she doesn't know what it is, she'll call Dad. Dad will know. And he'll say, 'Hum. Falsecium abidebyme. That would sure blow a toilet bowl all to hell.'"

"Right," I said. "So, let's do the window."

Skeet walked over to his window and pulled out the screen. He reached under his bed and came up with a roll of fishing line. He quickly tied a length of line around the jar, the line forming a cradle. He lowered the jar out the window. Once it was safely on the ground, Skeet looked at me.

"OK," I said, "see ya later." I bounded down the stairs, said "Bye" to the Barths, cut across the lawn, through my kitchen door, said "Hi" to my folks, ran up the stairs, and into my room. I pulled the screen out of my window, and Skeet threw the roll of line to me. I pulled the jar up through my window, untied it, rolled up the line, and tossed it back to Skeet. I had my own roll of line under my bed. "See you after supper," I said. We put our screens back and I hid the falsecium between my bed and nightstand for the time being. After that, I went downstairs to eat.

"Mr. Barth was just on the phone," Dad said after we had prayed. He said it casually, just before slipping a fork full of cooked carrots into his mouth. He looked over at me. I was chewing. It was not uncommon for Mr. Barth to call.

"What did he want?" I asked when I was done chewing. It was a serious question, not just polite conversation. Mr. Barth called often, but seldom socially. If he called it was generally to report mishaps and mysteries in which he had postulated Skeet and I where involved.

"Somehow," Dad continued, stifling a laugh, "he blew up his toilet."

I laughed, too. Just enough. Just enough to show I saw the humor in the situation, but not enough to suggest I was involved. I said, "I know. I was there when it happened. He said he threw his cigarette into the bowl and...."BOOOM! CRASH! THUMP! We all cringed. I swallowed hard. The noise had come directly from above the kitchen table. That would place the catastrophe somewhere in the vicinity of my bedroom. "Gosh," I choked, "I wonder what that was. Maybe our toilet blew up. I'd better go check." I got up.

"I'll go with you," Dad said.

"Bil," my mother said, "whatever you two boys are up too, we'll figure it out."

"Yes Ma'am," I said respectfully.

Dad and I walked upstairs. Just for show, I looked in the bathroom. The toilet had not exploded. I opened my bedroom door. It smelled a lot like asettling gas. The lamp on my bedside table was knocked over. It had fallen on my desk and upset a heavy glass mug I used to hold pens. The mug had fallen off the desk and onto the floor. There was a tape covered canning jar lid stuck in the heavy paper of the lampshade.

"Son," my dad said, "if you can tell me why I smell asettling gas in your room I won't kill you. If you can convince me it is for a good, constructive reason, I might let you keep the falsecium abidebyme. If you can tell me all that in the next fifty seconds, I won't tell your mom. But you'll be buying a toilet for Mr. Barth, no matter what."

"What?" I asked, incredulous.

"Now you have forty seconds."

"We got it to go in the falsecium lamps we bought. We were going to go caving. I put some in a canning jar to bring over here. Before we put it in the canning jar, we washed the jar out. I guess we didn't dry it completely. Then we taped the lid on."

"Why did you tape the lid on?"

I looked at Dad like he was nuts. I wanted to say "Duh!" but I refrained. Instead, I said, almost sarcastically, "So it wouldn't fall off." To myself I thought, "What a stupid question."

"Oh," Dad said, "for a second I thought you might be getting bright. I thought maybe you taped it on because you thought maybe, just maybe, some gas would build up in the jar and if you had screwed the lid on, instead of taping it on, the jar might explode, glass and all, because there would be no other way for the gas to escape. I thought you had reasoned the whole thing out and had included a bit of a safety release, if you will. Can you imagine what a mess that glass jar exploding would have made?

"Oh," was all I could say.

"Did the falsecium come in a can, like a paint can?"

"Yes."

"With a lid that you have to tap on?"

"Yes."

"Can you figure out why?"

I thought for a second. "In case the contents get wet and gas builds up? That way just the lid will blow off, instead of the can blowing up?"

"See, you aren't completely stupid, are you?"

"Not completely," I agreed.

"All right, let's go eat supper. You tell your mother exactly what happened. We'll let you keep the falsecium abidebyme. Then we'll call Mr. Barth and you can explain how and when you are going to fix his toilet."

That was about the best I could hope for. I wasn't really in trouble and I learned something that fit nicely with what we had gleaned from Mr. Barth tossing his butt into a toilet full of asettling. Namely, if you let the gas build up inside the can it would eventually blow the lid off. That gave me an idea.

After dinner, Dad and I went over to the Barths. Mr. Barth and Skeeter led us back to the bathroom where Skeet and I explained how the toilet came to be so explosive. Dad and Mr. Barth thought it was pretty funny, but not so funny that Skeet or I dared to join in the laughing. It was agreed that Skeet and I would buy a new toilet lid in the morning to replace the one we had caused to be busted.

The two of us went up to Skeet's room after that and retrieved the remaining can of falsecium. I detailed to Skeet what had happened with the canning jar in my bedroom. He looked intent as I described the principles my dad had explained. When I was done talking, Skeet simply stared at me. And then he smiled.

"What?" I asked.

"A boy could build a heck of a bazooka with a can of this stuff, a two-by-four, and some strong tape."

I smiled, too."

Deerly Departed

By Paul Lepp

I've never been much of a hunter, or perhaps I should say, I've never done much hunting. I know several fellas who aren't much of a hunter, and they hunt all the time. There have been times when I have occupied deer camps, though usually in the capacity of Chief Cook and Bottle Drainer. The camaraderie and closeness of a good deer camp is enough to warm the cockles of the heart and singe the hair of the nostrils. The food's pretty good too, if I do say so myself.

"Hey Charlie, pass me another opossum biscuit, and maybe a slab of weasel. Yep, muh doctor says I should eat lots of weasel, it's the other yellow meat, ya know."

"Say, ain't that venison jerky?"

"Naw, it was, but it's just quiverin' now."

Suffice it to say, I am familiar with hunters. I know that hunters are just as prone, if not as skillful, as anglers are to bending the truth. Still, I was taken aback to hear my normally game-law abiding friends brag of the massive number of deer they had taken in the recent seasons. I know that deer populations are at an all time high, and bag limits are liberal, but just the same, when my pal Fifty-Six Milkhouse proudly proclaimed around a mouthful of chipmunk dumpling that he had taken twenty-seven deer to date, this season, I suspected flagrant disregard not only of the truth, but also the truth.

This created a dilemma. Fact is, I'd much rather be between the horns of the largest, most raging dilemma on the earth than tangle with Fifty-six Milkhouse. If Fifty-Six is not his real name, no one, including his mother, knows what it is. It is a perfect name.

It was the number he wore when he decapitated eleven quarterbacks in his college team's perfect 10-0 season. He might have gone pro if one of the Q.B.'s hadn't been on his team. He shoots a .56 caliber rifle and carries a pistol of the same caliber as a backup. It's his chest size, too. About the only safe way to cross him is from at least 1,500 yards downwind.

I opted for diplomacy.

"Fifty-six," I said, "you see them two Dutch ovens in the coals over there? They're filled with your two favorite desserts. One is gobbler cobbler, the other is innards pie. If you are telling the truth, and account for each of those twenty-seven deer this year, and if you can tell us how you did it legal like, you can have all of both of 'em." This form of diplomacy, I believe, is what General George Patton referred to as "French Diplomacy." That is, no threat spoken, implied, or intended. It worked, too.

Fifty-six unlaced his boots, kicked them off, and peeled himself out of his socks. Plopping his big feet on the table he cracked his knuckles, and thus, calculator ready, began to cipher.

The first seven, he explained, were "gimmies," standard D.N.R.-authorized take. They were: gun, bow, black powder, pistol, knife and tomahawk. I was unable to locate the last three categories in the D.N.R. rules brochure, but Fifty-Six assured me I must be missing a page. Even so, that left twenty deer unaccounted for.

Wading in with obvious pride and enthusiasm he

ticked them off, first on his fingers, then on his toes. One jumped into the path of a bullet as he took aim at a dove. Similarly, two others got between him and a squirrel. When I inquired as to why he was hunting small game with a fifty-six-caliber rifle, he replied that he was out of all other kinds of ammo. Ten down, seventeen to go.

He took two with a truck, quite accidentally. In one instance, he stated that he had swerved nearly a hundred feet into the woods in an unsuccessful attempt to miss a ten-point buck. The dog drug in three. Fifty-Six owned a very ambitious toy poodle. One deer he did not see until he ran over it with the lawn mower, and although an unfortunate occurrence, one that saved a lot of time with skinning and butchering. That made sixteen.

Some of the deer fell victim to freak seasonal activities. In the spring, Fifty-Six told me, a large doe had somehow become entangled in his kite string and had strangled before Fifty-Six could save her. In the summer, on three occasions, hapless deer blundered into the pit he'd dug to install a swimming pool. Fifty-Six was distraught over this since they, too, had strangled before he could save them and thus he could not bring himself to complete the pool. Well, that and the fact that he couldn't find a pool kit that was fifteen feet deep, six feet wide and eight-feet long. In the winter a deer somehow mistook a bright red, cast iron ball for an apple, got his tongue stuck to it, and froze to death. Fifty-Six was unsure how the cast iron ball came to be painted red, how it happened to get mixed in with a basket of real apples, or how the bushel got left in the middle of the yard. But anyway, that deer made twenty-one.

I must admit, when he accounted for one as the victim of his chainsaw, I was skeptical. In my mind's eye, I just could not picture this guy in blaze orange, chasing a deer through the woods with a screaming, spitting, fuming chainsaw, and even if I could, I failed to believe that any deer (except maybe the frozen one) would stand still for it. Ah, but it was not like that at all, Fifty-Six assured me. Actually, he had been innocently cutting firewood when a large hickory tree coincidentally crossed a game trail precisely as an eight-pointer did also. Twenty-two.

One deer died of a broken neck after running into a barn door. This was an understandable accident on the deer's part as there was no barn attached to the door to slow it down as it fell from the tree.

Two more, Fifty-Six swears, just walked into his yard and keeled over, the apparent victims of massive coronaries. I thought the odds of that happening not just once, but twice, were rather long. Fifty-Six pointed out that there are millions of deer in the world. Some of them naturally suffered heart attacks, knowing as they did, very little about cholesterol and such. If they were going to die of heart attacks, he reasoned, his yard was as good a place as any.

Number twenty-six was taken with a golf ball at one hundred and twenty yards. It had no business in that sand trap to begin with, Fifty-Six said.

The twenty-seventh and final deer of the year (to date) was a forlorn, lovesick buck, spurned by a doe he cared for, who wandered into Fifty-Six's den, happened upon a loaded twelve gauge and ended its misery with the muzzle to its head and its hoof on the trigger. Fifty-Six said it ruined the rack, but the meat was still good.

You will notice that Fifty-Six stated that this was the last one to date. Actually, I was glad to hear him say that because now that it has been so reasonably explained to me, I'd like to take a shot at this fascinating sport. It appears I'm in luck, too, as my pal volunteered to take me out to his place next weekend to accompany him on the opening day of blowgun, spear, and dynamite season.

The Stealth Catfish

By Paul Lepp

There has been a lot of talk lately about Stealth bombers and fighters, what with Congressional budget hearings, military cutbacks, and elections. What few people realize, however, is that just as General Chuck Yeager, the world's greatest test pilot, originated in good ol' West Virginia, so too did Stealth technology. Oddly enough, the original Stealth concept did not even apply to aircraft, but instead to a particular creature known to scientists as *Ictalurus Furcatus*, and to anglers as the Blue Catfish.

Yes, hard as it may be to believe, my buddy Charlie and I modestly conceived, designed and implemented the first Stealth anything, and all for the benefit of my shift commander's swimming pool. From the day A.E. first filled his pool it had been beset with cats (the feline variety) who came to drink from its pristine waters. Evidently, word was mistakenly out among the cat world that the waters of A.E.'s pool harbored some type of feline medicinal value, just as the famed baths of White Sulphur Springs are supposed to do for humans. Whatever the reason, the pool attracted more cats than Nine Lives Tuna Surprise. Cats of every race, creed, and color flocked to partake.

Not only did the waters not hold any medicinal

cures, but once A.E. was aware of the situation, it became downright unhealthy for the cats to be caught at the pool. Maybe if it had just been the cat from next-door slipping over now and again for a few shots, A.E. wouldn't have minded, especially if he hadn't known about it. But when every cat from Clendenin to Cleveland began making regular pilgrimages to what was becoming a feline holy shrine, something had to be done. There were hairballs in the filters, catfights on the deck, and yowling day and night.

When A.E. was at the veritable peak of one of his anti-cat tirades, pacing the pool's length and screaming curses and damnation on every cat from Puss in Boots to Tony the Tiger, Charlie and I showed up to go fishing off his dock (the house sits on the Kanawha River). Through his rants we deciphered the situation and then slipped down to the dock to fish and ponder. The act of fishing, as anyone experienced will tell you, is inherently conducive to pondering. We discussed and dismissed many solutions to A.E.'s cat problem, ranging from live wires, to bear traps, to snares. Each of those ideas had their obvious drawbacks and so we had just settled on the idea of a cat trotline when a big fish hit.

It was a dandy. Even with the Monster Stick it took nearly half an hour to land him. He was a bit bigger than your average Kanawha River Blue Cat, weighing in at nearly sixty pounds. And he had a mouth like a basketball hoop. We were discussing what that fish could, and probably would, eat when it suddenly dawned on us— this was a CATfish. It undoubtedly could, and probably would, eat cats. Fish in hand, we headed up the bank.

The hour was late and A.E. had already turned in for the night. The cats, of course, were present in droves. They gave us a wide berth as we paraded our leviathan poolside. In we plunked him and stood watching as he slowly sank to the bottom. Then we retreated to observe. For a while, the fish lay like an old, submerged log, and gradually the cats returned to the water's edge.

The term "Blue Catfish" is something of a misnomer. Actually, they are more of a battleship gray in color, so our fish's outline was plainly visible against the sky blue liner of the well-lit pool. The four-footed cats eyed him warily, jumping in unison at the slightest movement. Obviously, a seek and destroy mission for our new anti-cat catfish would be difficult at best. What we needed was a system that would allow our boy to slip in undetected, underneath the feline cats' sensory perception network, thus allowing the fish to strike before any effective countermeasures could be taken. We needed mobile camouflage. In a word, we needed Stealth.

The plan we struck upon was beautiful in its simplicity. With a stout length of rope we lassoed the rascal back up out of the water and dumped him in the hot tub. Adding a quart of blue food coloring, we turned on the jets and let the big fella' stew until he was bluer than Paul Bunyan's famous ox. Then we tossed him back into the pool.

The transformation was startling. There was a splash as we dumped him in, but then he was gone. We rubbed our eyes and strained to make him out. Finally, we located what looked like two black marbles, about a foot apart, cruising horizontally just below the surface. As for the four-legged cats, well, they smelled a fish. That is to say, their curiosity was piqued, and we all know what curiosity does to a cat.

About the Stories

The Butti Mystery

This story developed out of a conversation at work about whether or not *Yet* and *But* are synomous. That conversation stemmed from a sermon I heard wherein the preacher constantly substituted the word *Yet* for *But*. How did Bigfoot get involved? Well, the story started quickly one day with Skeet and I in the tent, frozen to the floor, and then went nowhere for a long time. I finally figured out that if I could put us in that tent for a reason, I might get a story out of it. That's where 'But,' 'Yet,' the Yeti, and Bigfoot entered the ordeal.

Thinking Behind

Up to a point, this is a true tale. I did get one of my cars stuck in the mud, and I did pull it out with our Jeep. I did suddenly realize that yard was far steeper than I would have thought, and I did have quite a time stopping the two cars from meeting each other in a mutually disagreeable way.

The Ultra-Secret Advanced Armadillo Reconnaissance Unit

Often, my stories get finished and then I struggle for a title. This story started as a title struggling for a story. I thought of the title while sitting in the dark

Mississippi night, waiting for armadillos, and then thought, "I oughta write this all down." Sometimes life is like that.

Vanity PL8

I was asked to tell stories at my buddy's wedding. He is from West Virginia, his bride from California. I decided I would write a story that offended both sets of guests. I wrote a piece that described the history of both West Virginia and California in unflattering, but funny, terms. I also made fun of my buddy's truck. The only person offended by the tale, as it turned out, was my buddy's mechanic. The same truck has shown up in a few of my stories, but here it comes into its own. This story was also sparked by an ever-so-inspired idea to get myself a vanity plate for my car that read, obviously, VANITY PL8. It's too long for a West Virginia plate, and I expect compensation if I see any of you driving around another state with the tag.

Avant Garden

I've always liked the idea of doing commentary for public radio. Every so often I write a piece and submit it. They always get rejected. This is one of those short pieces. I believe my father would agree with the description of gardening technique.

Something in the Water

I wrote this story a couple of years ago. I can't remember why.

Fat Bats

I make a habit of listening to other people's conversations. I know it is not polite, but now and then I will hear things like, "...Yep, the cicadas were bad that year, but Lord, we had some fat bats flying around." It took me about an hour to write this story. Sometimes simple statements are stories unto their own, and you need simply stretch them.

Naaman and the Hiccups

I was listening to a sermon on this passage and couldn't help but think that it would be far more relevant if Naaman had the hiccups, instead of leprosy. And there you have it. The rest is just biblical plagiarism.

Artist's Renderings

The Lepp family has had a tenuous relationship with the military establishment in general. My grandfather's people were Mennonites, and thus pacifists. This did not stop my grandfather from fighting with the White Army in the Russian Revolution. He fled the country. My brother, Paul, served as a Military Policeman, and made it through without being arrested himself. My Uncle Paul went to college, and thus Vietnam, via ROTC. He had no intention of being a career officer. This story is, more or less, true.

The Fall of Babble-On

Another attempt at biblical storytelling. Guess the book? Read Revelation. I'd be interested to see what you think.

Quantity 4: Quality 0

I've tried to tell this story a few times, but it just doesn't work well aloud. I had a friend named Mike when I was growing up, and we used to build airplanes in his garage. You will, I hope, begin to recognize in my tales where the truth stops and the lie starts.

My buddy Mike and I never actually tried to fly one of our planes. My stories generally begin at the point where common sense prevailed in real life, and our airplane making, dressing up like deer, tying myself to dogs, etc., became recorded forever as untried, bad ideas. My stories explore the "what if" of my childhood endeavors, but exist in a place where broken bones, hurt feelings, and wrong choices have no consequence but humor.

Stop Sign Man

My son came up with this concept. Somewhere in his toddler mind he invented Stop Sign Man as a way of stopping people from approaching him. If I was walking toward him to say, tickle him, and he did not want to be tickled, he would hold his hand in front him, palm out, and yell, "STOP SIGN MAN!" Eventually, he began asking Paula and me to tell him stories about Stop Sign Man fighting pirates, dragons, and so on.

A Ride in the Pinpricked Hyphen

I call this sort of story Extended Commentary. I was, in fact, nearly drowned in a kayak. It was not the kayak's fault, but I still blame the event on other factors . . . factors other than myself, that is. So, I figured I'd write the story so that I could broadcast my views on kayaking, men in skirts, and things of that general ilk. A lot of times I think of something, or say something, on one subject or another, and then think, "I gotta use that in a story." When I have enough of these ideas stored up dealing with one subject or another, but still no tale, I will generally produce one of these Extended Commentaries simply as a vehicle to express my pent-up ideas.

The Art of No-Hope Fishing

I have found that most often I catch fish when I am least expecting to. For example, when you prop your rod on the edge of the boat, let go for only second, just to grab a coke out of the cooler, the next sound you hear will be the pole splashing into the water. If you are lucky, you see the pole as it sinks out of sight. So, this story simply expands that idea.

Jonah, The Last Two Chapters

At long last, I have finished my version of the Jonah story which first showed up in *The Monster Stick*, from August House. In my first version of the story, I leave Jonah spit out of the fish, but really directionless. Here, at last, I bring him to Nineveh and the theological meat of the tale.

Dimes

You think I'm kidding, but when I was kid I did figure that it would be easier to become a millionaire by dimes, rather than dollars. I did end up with dimes all over my floor, but the law was never really involved.

Animal Escort

Every morning I get up and try to write the storytelling equivalent of Bruce Springsteen's *Thunder Road*. More often than not, I end with a Rick Springfield B side. Nevertheless, I like this story. I think that when I finally get around to telling it on stage it will flesh out a bit, but we'll see.

Of Chicken Wieners and Fathers-in-Law

I had to figure out a way to brag about the fact that my father-in-law caught a thirty-pound catfish using chicken wieners, and I wanted someone to believe me. This is true stuff.

Engine Blockhead
Ever done something really stupid? Write it down.

Falsecium Abidebyme - Part I?
There is a Part II, but you'll have to read my eventually to be completed novel to find out what it is. This is one of stories, like *Mayhem Dressed Like an Eight Point Buck*, in which I hope to combine elements of the tall-tale with more classic literary elements. I hope this is a story that you can believe, and through which you might glean a bit about that old cuss the Human Condition, but you can also just enjoy the sheer folly of it all.

Deerly Departed
and
Stealth Catfish
These two stories were submitted as part of my first book, *The Monster Stick and Other Appalachian Stories*, from August House Press, but they didn't make the final cut. They are both by my brother, and two of my favorites.

About the Author

Bil Lepp has been a featured storyteller at the National Storytelling Festival, the Smithsonian Folklife Festival and numerous other events around the country. Five-time winner of the West Virginia Liar's Contest, he is a popular presenter and keynote speaker at festivals, corporate events, colleges, schools, and other organizations. He also conducts workshops and seminars on learning how to "lie" well.

Bil's two previous books are *Inept: Impaired: Overwhelmed* and *The Monster Stick.* You can listen to Bil tell his stories on his two CD's—*Mayhem Dressed Like an Eight Point Buck* and *Buck Dog Meets the Monster Stick.*

Bil resides in South Charleston, WV, with his wife and two children, Noah and Ellie, both of whom appear to be following in their father's storytelling footsteps.

Please visit Bil at his website www.buck-dog.com.